The Post Box Topper Chronicles

The Post Box Topper Chronicles

Dawn Knox

Chapeltown Books

British Library Cataloguing in Publication Data
A Record of this Publication is available from the British Library

ISBN 978-1-915762-12-2

This edition published 2024 by Chapeltown Books
Manchester, England

Contents

The Post Box Topper Outrage

The sender of the email was A. Godbin.

Vera Twinge didn't recognise the name. She was most particular about emails. If she didn't know the sender, she simply consigned the unopened message to the bin, having learnt all about spam and the germs it carried. She'd twice clicked on links in a strange email, resulting in an infected computer – and a large bill from her IT guru-ess, Amrita.

But the email from A. Godbin had the subject line, 'Post Box Topper Outrage', and Vera hadn't been able to resist opening it.

As she read, a slow scream gathered in her throat. How dare he… or she – or in this society with its surfeit of political correctness – how dare they?

A. Godbin certainly had a nerve, whatever his, her or their gender. Vera rummaged through her well-organised brain, but she was certain there was no one in Creaping Bottom by that name. It was only a small village, and she knew everyone, as well as members of their extended families. She even knew the names of their houses and their pets.

Unable to believe it, Vera reread the message.

> *Dear Mrs Twinge,*
>
> *I am emailing regarding the recent outrage that you and your club, The Creaping Bottom Post Box Topper Society, perpetrated on the letterbox in the*

High Road last weekend. I understand from passers-by that it is supposed to represent January and that you intend to commit a similar outrage on the village's only letterbox each month for the rest of the year. I have no idea what a cow pat, a squashed insect and sleeping chicken have to do with January. I suspect this owes more to an inflated idea of your artistic abilities than to a desire to serve our community. I dread to think how you might massacre February and subsequent months.

I have reported the disgrace to the local constabulary; however, I do not feel they have treated my complaint with the seriousness it deserves. Be assured, I will not rest until the matter has been fully investigated and dealt with to my satisfaction. The police inspector is a member of the local golf club of which I am a committee member, and I am confident he will agree with me that the offending article must be removed with all haste.

Of course, you could save me the trouble and simply remove the eyesore yourself and desist from further installations. I would be most grateful.

Yours,

A. Godbin.

Vera stared at the email for several minutes. Yes, it definitely said what she'd thought it said the first time she'd read it. She pressed the Forward button and entered the names of the four other members of the Creaping Bottom Post Box Topper Society.

Petronella Asquelch, Stuart McPhail, Sally Bobbin and Levi von Regenschirm.

She pressed the Send button. A. Godbin's offensive email left her inbox with a *whoosh.*

'The club had started as a knit-and-natter group but Vera had decided against knitting boring squares. She'd had the idea of knitting post box toppers and had suggested they make one to decorate the post box outside the Post Office in the High Road as a Christmas project.

Vera had crocheted the bonnet, which fitted snugly over the top. After purchasing a hardcover copy of *The Anatomy of the British Pillar Box,* she discovered the top was referred to as the 'roof' by post box enthusiasts. Now, she was thoroughly conversant with all anatomical terms relating to post boxes.

The other items for the topper – two snowmen and a Christmas tree – should have been fixed on the roof. However, although the crocheted bonnet had been straightforward, the other items proved to be infinitely more complicated. Eventually, after they'd produced eleven mutant snowmen and five Christmas bushes, they'd agreed their effort wouldn't be ready in time.

Nothing daunted, Vera knew there were months

in which to hone their skills before next Christmas to ensure the snowmen and Christmas tree looked… well, as realistic as woollen snowmen and trees could be.

Levi von Regenschirm had practised knitting a menorah for next December, creating a multi-faith theme. While Vera offered Levi encouraging platitudes, she consoled herself with the knowledge there were still months for him to practise. She certainly didn't want to discourage him for fear he'd think she was discriminating against Hanukkah. But he was going to have to find a way to stiffen the arms of the menorah candelabrum.

His earlier attempts had given poor Sally quite a turn. Levi had flapped it up and down, demonstrating the drooping arms of the candelabrum. He'd done an admirable job of exhibiting their floppiness, but had been completely unprepared for Sally's response. Her scream had reached the Creaping Arms pub, where patrons had hurried into the High Road, fearing a murder had taken place. As Sally had explained after they'd picked her up off the floor and Vera had wafted smelling salts under her nose, Levi's menorah had looked remarkably like a hairy-legged spider.

Vera was determined that by the end of the year, the group would be able to create convincing snowmen, Christmas trees and a menorah. Possibly even some holly, crackers and an angel. She'd wondered about an entire Nativity Scene, but perhaps that should wait until the following Christmas… In the meantime, they'd concentrate on her latest project.

Such had been the enthusiasm; the January post box topper had been finished rapidly – in fact, it probably took longer to decide what to make than to actually create the pieces. They'd planned to knit the letters to spell out January, but 'J', 'A' and 'N' had proved so tricky, they'd decided to stop there.

Stuart had suggested that since Burns Night took place in January, he'd like to make a set of bagpipes and a haggis. Petronella had done her very best with a cockerel on a weathervane and a puffy, rain-bearing cloud to show the storms that were often experienced during the month. And the entire topper had looked splendid.

So, how could he – Vera was certain that A. Godbin was a *he* – how could he possibly have confused the haggis, bagpipes and weathervane with a cow pat, a squashed insect and a sleeping chicken? Although, to be fair, the cockerel listed to one side and didn't look too lively. Had the stupid man thought the cloud was a pillow? No, surely not. It was obviously a cumulo-nimbus. Everyone knew gales blew in January. As for the cow pat… Vera had never seen one so… well, so *well-formed*. On the other hand, she'd never seen a haggis either. But a tartan insect? No, A. Godbin obviously didn't possess even a modicum of imagination.

And anyway, what else could they have chosen?

January didn't contain many major events. And it wasn't many people's favourite month. Even the dismal grey wool she'd chosen for the bonnet – which she noted with satisfaction, A. Godbin hadn't criticised – told its own story.

Ping.

A reply to the forwarded email arrived in her inbox from Levi. It contained a single word – not a word she approved of, or ever used. She wouldn't fill up her computer with vulgarity. Vera deleted his email. But she'd got the message.

The others would reply soon. Well, if A. Godbin thought she'd give up, he'd better think again. February's post box topper was going to be an extravaganza.

If A. Godbin wanted a fight, Vera was ready. Let the Creaping Bottom Post Box Topper Wars begin. She rubbed her hands together. *Bring it on…*

Post Box Topper Surveillance

Vera Twinge rubbed two circles – side by side – in the condensation on the café window. The four other members of the Creaping Bottom Post Box Topper Society who were seated at the table with her stopped knitting to watch. Leaning towards the window, Vera peered through the two clear spots into the street.

'Can you see anything?' whispered Petronella.

Vera shook her head. 'I made the circles too far apart and I can't see through them both at the same time.'

'Shall I make some?' Stuart raised his hand to rub two more circles in the misty glass.

'Certainly not! We're on secret surveillance. We don't want the culprit to see us. If lots of clear spots suddenly appear in the condensation, it'll look rather obvious, like a lot of owls blinking in a dark barn.'

Vera pressed her nose to the glass and peered through one of her spyholes. 'The rain's coming down in stair rods now and I can't see anything. But the good news is I think we can safely assume no one's going to interfere with our post box topper while the weather's so bad.'

'That means we can enjoy our tea and buns… and each other's company.' Sally glanced sideways at Levi and blushed so deeply her cheeks matched the red wool she was knitting.

Vera sighed. She wished Sally wasn't so obvious in her adoration of Levi. It was undignified.

The Creaping Bottom Post Box Topper Society had moved from the community hall to Bonzer Buns next to the Post Office on the High Road. They intended to protect the new February post box topper they'd lovingly positioned on top of the pillar box outside. Of course, they couldn't monitor it twenty-four hours a day, seven days a week, but Beryl, proprietor of Bonzer Buns, had offered to help. In exchange for them swapping their venue for her coffee and cake shop, she'd offered to spy for them when they weren't there. And better still, she had a CCTV camera in the café positioned in such a way that it could also see into the street, including the post box and its magnificent topper.

Sadly, since Vera had agreed to change venues, the CCTV camera had been on the blink and hadn't produced any useful footage. But Beryl assured her the technician was due any day. Just as well, because a saboteur had struck on several occasions, removing many of the knitted hearts on the February Valentine display. And no one had witnessed the act. They'd spent ages deciding on the February display. And now to know it had been vandalised was heart-breaking.

Vera had crocheted the bonnet which fitted over the roof of the post box. January's had been dull grey, but this one was red – the colour associated with Valentine's Day. And everyone had spent hours knitting hearts. They'd sewn them together and stuffed them to make tiny, heart-shaped cushions which had been arranged in an artful design and attached to the red bonnet. Accompanying them was a profusion of red and pink knitted roses and ribbons.

Stuart had been responsible for the roses which, Vera acknowledged silently, bore very little resemblance to flowers, and were more like miniature cabbages. But luckily, no one had mentioned this to him. He was rather prickly when it came to criticism.

Once the topper had been completed, the members of the group had taken selfies and congratulated themselves. However, the following day Vera received a complaint via email from the mysterious A. Godbin.

She was still certain A. Godbin was male, and his message gave her no reason to suspect otherwise.

Snooty and snotty. That's what Vera thought about his email. It had been written in similar tones to the message she'd received from him in January. This time, he'd been just as disagreeable. He'd requested – no, *demanded* – she remove the topper. He'd previously described the January topper as an 'outrage'. Apparently, he considered the February creation a 'downright disgrace' and 'a blot on the Creaping Bottom High Road'.

How could anyone object to a Valentine's Day celebration? Where was the man's heart?

He obviously didn't have one. But if he had, and if Vera had known where it was, she'd have ripped it out and added it to the display. Especially when they'd discovered some hearts had gone missing. Oddly, none of the roses had disappeared, and Stuart had been most relieved. Vera was grateful no one had put forward a plausible explanation for this.

Luckily, they were able to replace the missing hearts with spare ones. There could be no doubt who the culprit was, and so Vera had called this extraordinary meeting in Bonzer Buns to prevent further sabotage.

Who knew when A. Godbin would strike again? But if he did, The CBPBTS would be ready – well, during Beryl's opening hours, anyway.

However, as a secret surveillance operation, the extraordinary meeting had failed. Despite being Saturday, any hardy souls who were out shopping had deserted the rain-sodden High Road and had gathered in Bonzer Buns for Beryl's delicious coffee and homemade cakes. Such a crush of people, with their wet dogs and damp coats, ensured the large window where the society members sat was running with condensation.

But it wasn't all bad. If the society members couldn't see the post box from their surveillance point, well, they could knit, chat, and plan future toppers. All in the cosy warmth of the café – with coffee and cake only a nod away. Beryl allowed them to remain at the large table in the window for as long as they liked and was going to charge them what she called 'mates' rates'. It was just as well. Vera had already lost count of how much they'd spent that day, and she was leaving it to the society's treasurer, Stuart, to settle the bill from their funds.

With all the money they'd saved when they'd cancelled their booking in the Creaping Bottom Community Centre, their finances would now stretch further. The room in the community centre was cold and uncomfortable. What's more, if you wanted a cup of coffee, you had to chip instant coffee granules out of the jar with a knife. But Bonzer Buns was warm and cosy – if currently a little damp, and Beryl served cakes and a variety of coffees – cappuccino, latte, Americano, and double or triple espresso, which was particularly useful for Levi. He was an artist who often forgot to go to bed at night if he was caught 'in the moment'. He was so tired the next day, he'd fall asleep, his head nodding perilously closer to his knitting needles until Sally jogged him with her elbow to prevent him from impaling himself. He usually brought himself round with a jolt of caffeine. But they'd have to think about raising more funds very soon.

Perhaps if they could attract new members… But that relied on good publicity, such as having an unmolested topper on display on the High Road for all to admire.

A. Godbin's sabotage attempts were not helping.

Vera had reported the vandalism at the local police station, but they weren't treating it as a priority. No, she knew she couldn't rely on the local constabulary. In his latest email, A. Godbin had once again mentioned he'd complained about the toppers to Detective Inspector Crimini, who, he reminded her, was a fellow member of the local golf club. Vera cared nothing for any arrangement between golf club members. If she caught A. Godbin in the act of sabotaging the February topper, she'd grab him by his scrawny neck and wring it like a chicken. That would put a stop to his nonsense.

'I think we're wasting our time keeping watch for the perpetrator,' Stuart said, staring forlornly at the opaque window. As ever, he was several beats behind everyone else.

Sally looked at him in alarm. 'Oh, surely, we shouldn't give up just yet…' she glanced at Levi from beneath her eyelashes, willing him to stay.

'Yes,' agreed Levi. 'I want another of Beryl's Canberra Cupcakes.'

Sally almost swooned with pleasure.

'So, any ideas for March's topper?' Vera asked briskly, with a surreptitious shake of her head at Sally's silliness.

'Well, we could make something to celebrate Mother's Day,' Petronella said.

Thank goodness for Petronella, thought Vera.

Such a sensible woman. But then you'd expect a librarian to be organised.

'And St. David's and St. Patrick's Days. We could knit leeks and shamrocks,' Levi said as he raised his hand to summon Beryl's teenage assistant, Tilly, to take his order.

'What about Pi Day?' Stuart ran his tongue over his upper lip to mop up the froth from his cappuccino. The action only pushed the residual foam further upwards to form a blond Dali-esque moustache.

'Any particular sort of pie?' Sally asked. 'Meat or fruit pie? Pork pie? Or just pies in general?'

'No, not pies. Pi. Mathematical Pi.'

There was silence for a few moments while they all tried to imagine – or, indeed, even remember – what mathematical Pi was.

'Trust you to think of that,' said Petronella. Her eyes narrowed. 'Mathematical Pi Day? Seriously? Are you sure you're not pulling our legs?'

'Absolutely not! It's on the fourteenth of March. A day to celebrate the wonder of mathematics.'

Levi yawned. His eyelids drooped and his knitting dangled from his hands.

'You're a typical accountant, Stuart,' Petronella said.

'I beg your pardon!' said Stuart. 'There's nothing wrong with accountancy—'

'Enough!' said Vera. 'If Stuart can think of something sensible that we can knit to represent Pi, then let's include it.'

'We could knit an apple pie,' said Levi sleepily. 'It could be a culinary interpretation of mathematical Pi. A sort of allegory—'

'Bunkum,' said Stuart. 'Apple pies never stood in for 3.1415—'

'Moving on,' said Vera quickly.

'Bunkum… Now, there's a thought. I wonder what colour bunkum is…' said Levi thoughtfully, his eyes almost shut.

'Such a superb imagination,' Sally said with a soppy smile on her face.

'It's Red Nose Day in March, isn't it?' Petronella said. 'That'll mean more red wool…'

Everyone except Levi, who was now studying the interior of his eyelids, looked down at the hearts they were knitting.

'Can we bear more red wool? It's giving me spots before the eyes,' Petronella said.

'Let's have lots of daffodils,' Sally said. 'That'll ring the changes. Yellow isn't as hard on the eyes as red.'

'Yes. Nothing says March like daffodils.'

'What else shall we have?' Vera asked.

Levi opened his eyes. 'If we're ordering, I'll have more coffee…'

'For goodness' sake, get him a triple espresso to go with that Canberra Cupcake he ordered, Sally, or we'll be carrying him home,' Vera said.

Sally leapt up and rushed to the counter.

Vera put her knitting down and wrote on her pad. 'I meant what other things could we make to represent March? So far, we've got daffodils, leeks, shamrocks, red noses and some sort of homage to Pi. Any more ideas?'

Petronella searched on her phone. 'World Book Day on the second of March…'

'We should be able to knit a book or two. Not red books, though.'

Stuart frowned at her. 'I'm not sure what you mean, Vera. You can't read knitted books. They're… well… knitted.'

Sometimes, Stuart was so dense, Vera thought crossly. 'I meant we shouldn't knit any books in red wool. Not that we shouldn't include any books in our display that had been read.' She sighed. It was like being whisked back twenty years to when she'd been in charge of a class of six-year-olds.

'Oh, here's a good one,' Petronella said. 'It's Barbie Day on the ninth of March. I've got an old Barbie doll somewhere in the loft. We could knit some clothes and use her.'

Sally rushed back to their table. 'I say! I just looked out of the door and our topper's been tampered with.'

It was true. Vera and the other members of the society gathered around the post box in the pouring rain and surveyed the topper. Hearts had been carefully clipped away and removed.

'When I get my hands on him…' Vera's voice was low and menacing. Her fists were clenched and they worked back and forth as if she was throttling something.

'Come on, let's go back inside. We're getting drenched and there's nothing we can do,' said Petronella, leading the way back into Bonzer Buns.

'What a shame,' said Beryl when she heard what had happened. 'More coffee and buns, everyone?'

The society members nodded.

'We will not be beaten,' Vera said, wiping the rain off her face with a tissue. 'I fear we must concede the first battle. But the Creaping Bottom Post Box Topper Wars are not over. However, we must change tactics. Subtlety does not appear to be working. We must be more overt.'

'I'm not standing outside in the rain being overt for anyone,' Petronella said. 'I'm just saying.'

'Oh, you're such a lightweight, Petronella,' said Levi with a smile. 'This is war, you know.'

Sally roared with laughter. 'Oh, Levi, you're so funny!'

Vera ground her teeth and frowned at Sally. 'We will simply wipe down the window and then we'll all be able to keep an eye on what's left until we can sew on more hearts. Secrecy is overrated. We will not be owls blinking in a dark barn. We'll floodlight the barn and then we'll see what's what.'

'Well, don't wipe the window with your tissues,'

Petronella said. 'When they get wet, they disintegrate… Like they've done on your face.'

Vera looked down at the mushy remains of the tissue, and her hands flew to her face to discover countless tiny scraps of soggy tissue sticking to her skin.

Later, after a trip to the ladies to wash her face, she reappeared to find Tilly Dawkins, Beryl's part-time employee, scowling at the society members as she wiped the condensation off the window with a cloth.

What a sulky teenager she was. How on earth did Beryl put up with her?

Vera surveyed her troops. Levi was asleep. Sally was trying to rescue his upturned needles without waking him as his chin dropped closer to them. Stuart had put his glasses on and was poring over the list he'd made of all the cups of coffee and buns they'd consumed. And Petronella was alternately knitting furiously and peering at the post box outside. Ah, bless her. Vera could rely on Petronella. If they really had been troops, Petronella would have earned her sergeant's stripes.

Outside Bonzer Buns, unnoticed by the members of the CBPBTS, stood sixteen-year-old Shane Fowle. He was drenched through but would have been willing to go through flood, fire or pestilence – had he known what that was – for the love of his life, Tilly Dawkins.

Not that his love was returned. So far, she was playing hard to get. Very hard to get.

But he'd win her over. After all, how many other boys were standing outside in the rain waiting to walk her home?

None. Just him.

And one day, she'd recognise his devotion. She'd already spotted him when she'd cleaned the windows a few moments ago. He thought she'd been smiling at him, although he couldn't be sure. For a smile, it was a bit intense. But intensity was good, wasn't it? Love was passionate.

He put his hand in his pocket and moved the penknife to one side to feel the knitted hearts he'd just found on the post box. It was a shame they were drenched. He gave them another squeeze, soaking his pocket further. Oh well, they'd dry out, eventually. Although his jacket was now so wet, the hearts were becoming more sodden – if that was possible. He frowned. The Valentine's card in his pocket might be too soggy to give her, but he was sure she'd find the hearts romantic. For a second, he wondered whether to go back to the post box and liberate some of those red and pink coiled things, but decided against it. He wasn't sure what they were, and they had a sort of snail vibe. No, perhaps he'd leave them. The hearts said it all.

Yes, he had a good feeling about his chances with Tilly tonight.

Post Box Topper Confusion

Going home time.

Tilly Dawkins wiped the last of the tables in Beryl's café, studiously ignoring the aggravating boy outside.

The foul Shane Fowle. Outside in the cold, wet, dark street.

With hands cupped around his face, he pressed them against the window.

Wipe, wipe.

Ignore, ignore.

Shane had taken to tapping on the glass. Tilly increased the volume on her AirPods and with one final exaggerated sweep of the table – and a wiggle of her bottom to keep him interested, she'd walked back to the sink. She glanced in the mirror to reassure herself he was still there, then with a flick of her wrist, she switched off the lights, plunging the cosy café into darkness.

Beryl let Tilly out of the back door and went upstairs to her flat. Tilly walked home, avoiding the High Road where Shane Fowle stood waiting and tapping.

And pining.

His heart was broken, and the pilfered woollen hearts in his hand, sopping wet.

The following morning, Effie Wiggins, the cleaner, arrived at Bonzer Buns early as usual. Never was a woman better suited to her job. Effie could not abide dirt and disorder.

She started in the kitchen. That didn't take long because Beryl always left it tidy when she finished each day. The café, however, usually required attention because Tilly didn't have an eye for detail. Not that she didn't notice dirt. She did. But rather than clear it up, she swept it into places she thought Effie wouldn't find it.

Stupid girl.

Effie had seek-and-destroy capabilities when it came to grime.

She waddled across the floor, heaving her vast bulk and her set of cleaning tools in her arms. WOMD. Weapons of Mess Destruction. Effie's arsenal looked like an armful of bizarre, fluffy and bristly golf clubs. A cleaning tool was not a cleaning tool unless it had an extendible pole.

Effie did not do bending or stretching.

Mops and brooms came with long handles, but Effie also had squeegees, feather dusters, brushes, and dustpans – all attached to extendible poles.

Minimal reaching required.

Effie turned the lights on and glanced about, assessing what needed to be done. She halted and gaped at the red mess on the mat.

Adjusting her spectacles, she waddled towards it; a broom outstretched. Liquid oozed from the red objects when she prodded them, and she stepped back with a gasp of horror.

They would have looked at home on Mr Snyde's butcher's slab. Or in a horror movie.

Effie sniffed the air and reached for the can of air freshener in the kangaroo pouch pocket of her apron. Thankfully, there was no tell-tale odour of decay. Good. She simply refused to permit unpleasant smells. She blasted the offending red articles with a squirt of summer haze, anyway.

Extending her long-handled brush towards the foul stuff, Effie was just about to use the trigger to open her long-handled dustpan and clear it away, when she had a dreadful thought. Those revolting squashed, red things lying on the doormat reminded her of a ghastly incident at her friend's house.

Slovenly, sloppy Gertie Funnell was an unlikely friend for fastidious Effie Wiggins. Whenever Effie visited, she took her cleaning arsenal with her. Gertie invited her around regularly and by the time Effie had left, the house would be spotless.

The filthiest thing about Gertie's house was Gwillum, a malevolent and mangy, feral cat, which came and went as it pleased. The previous month, Effie had been cleaning Gertie's windows when Gwillum had presented her with several gifts. Three mice lay on the kitchen doormat in a line next to a fledgling bird.

Effie awarded Gwillum full marks for neatness, then, feeling the bile rise in her throat, made her excuses, and hurried away without giving the windows a final buff. Before she'd left, she'd considered clearing the dead bodies, but hadn't wanted to contaminate her precious cleaning tools. And Effie was not going to bend over for anyone, particularly not Gwillum, so she'd left them on the mat.

Her lumbago twanged at the thought of shifting out of the vertical.

So, were these mushy things similar offerings? She decided to risk another poke with the broom. After all, it was already contaminated. The red stuff squelched. Effie stepped back further and made a mental note to clean her broom head later.

Who'd put them there? They were beneath the letterbox. Had someone posted them through there as an act of malevolence?

Mafia, perhaps?

Unlikely. Everyone loved Beryl and her buns.

Had she got a cat? No, not Beryl. She wouldn't allow one of those revolting creatures into her café. So, it must be something wild that had crept in.

Such as?

A rat? Or… Oh no!

When Effie had arrived that morning, she'd seen a squirrel run across the High Road. Was it possible?

Last year, to her absolute horror, she'd called in a man to investigate what she thought might be rats in her loft, only to find she had a squirrel infestation. Once the man had blocked all the holes and left,

Beryl had somehow prised herself up through the loft hatch and spent the day cleaning up. It was amazing what one determined woman could do with a vacuum cleaner and a long hose, even if it had blocked twice.

However, back to the problem. Squirrels were vindictive, vicious creatures with beady eyes and grasping claws. Yes, now Effie thought about it, that squirrel she'd seen earlier had regarded her with a shifty stare. There was no doubt, this mess was squirrel-related.

Well, she'd tell Beryl later. In the meantime, if those squirrels thought she was going to be intimidated, they'd better think again. She stepped forward and, with her trigger finger, opened the lid of the dustpan. She briskly swept the offending articles inside, allowing the lid to close with a satisfying *clunk*.

With the dexterity that comes with hours of practice, she transferred the contents of the dustpan into a large plastic bag and zipped the top up with a flourish. All without inclining her body more than a few degrees. She left the bag by the side of the bin as evidence to show Beryl when she came down.

Effie's mobile phone rang. She sighed when she saw the caller's identity. It was her brother.

'Hello, Des.' She paused to listen.

'Oh, honestly, Des! If I've told you once, I've told you a thousand times. You shouldn't let the budgie out. Where is it now?'

Pause. 'Well, I'm not surprised! Wouldn't you be flying around if someone was chasing you with a vacuum cleaner hose? You'll give the poor thing a heart attack! Beryl won't mind if I leave early. I'll come round. Turn off the vacuum cleaner. There's nothing worse than a blocked hoover.'

Pause. 'It's off? Good. And where's the budgie now? Good. Right, see you in a few minutes. Cheerio.'

Vera Twinge, chairperson of the Creaping Bottom Post Box Topper Society, arrived at nine o'clock, when Bonzer Buns opened. The four other members joined her shortly after. They took their usual table in the window, ready to keep vigil, watching the February post box topper. Hearts had disappeared regularly off the Valentine's-Day-themed display, but Stuart had been pleased his roses had remained unmolested. No one mentioned his knitted creations had been as similar to real roses as hobnail boots were to ballet shoes. Still, they'd only be on the post box for another week.

Vera stepped back in alarm. The press? What on earth would people think when they saw that photo? The humiliation! The society would be ruined.

Already, March's post box topper was almost complete. Today, they would knit the finishing touches, which would be attached with ultra-strong thread and wire to deter any interference. The Barbie doll in the centre, ready for Barbie Day on the ninth of March, had given most cause for concern.

Initially, Vera had a few sleepless nights imagining that someone might steal it – until she'd actually seen Petronella's old Barbie doll.

Many years before, a young Petronella had practised her hairdressing skills on the doll. The best that could be said was that it was fortunate Petronella had become a librarian.

Levi had made a rather fine Ascot-style hat, and he'd tucked what remained of the doll's hair up into it. The Biro tattoos gave Barbie a rather rugged, biker look, but the knitted clothes had hidden most of them.

And really, one had to take risks in life, didn't one? If Barbie disappeared, well, so be it. And Vera, for one, wouldn't be too disappointed.

The rest of the display consisted of leeks, shamrocks and a profusion of daffodils. Stuart's mathematical Pi had presented problems, but since it had only given Stuart problems, Vera hadn't been too concerned. He had, in the end, cleverly inserted wire into a knitted tube and fashioned something that looked like the Greek letter Pi. Most people would probably think it was some sort of triumphal arch, but that didn't really concern Vera. Stuart was pleased with it, and arguably, that was all that mattered.

To commemorate World Book Day, there were several knitted books with titles embroidered on them. Of course, they'd had to be choosy because embroidering Alice in Wonderland had resulted in such tiny stitches, it was illegible. They'd finally settled on Emma, Macbeth and Dracula. A strange selection, but it covered various genres and hadn't been too challenging to embroider.

The bonnet Vera had crocheted was green, which blended in with the fresh spring colour scheme. All in all, Vera was satisfied.

A frisson of excitement surged through her as she anticipated an email from A. Godbin as soon as the March topper was installed.

But would he email?

Vera would be disappointed if he didn't – even if she could then claim she'd won the Post Box Topper Wars. Winning was always a heady experience, but if A. Godbin just gave up, she'd feel like the general of an army who was waiting for an enemy that never arrived.

She was still no closer to knowing the mysterious emailer's identity, even though she'd carried out discreet enquiries. There were three golf clubs within a reasonable distance from Creaping Bottom. She'd enquired at the closest, but they'd claimed there was no A. Godbin on their books.

The second club she'd contacted had been very secretive – as if the first one had tipped them off. Vera was now investigating the most distant club. It was proving tricky. The obvious club was the one where Inspector Crimini belonged because A. Godbin had mentioned him. But he seemed to belong to all three. Was that possible? Vera didn't know. But no one would confirm anything. Well, she'd just have to persist.

Vera looked up and sighed. Sally had slipped into the seat next to Levi and was fussing over him in a very unseemly manner.

Where was that girl's self-respect? As usual, however, Levi was ignoring her. He must have had a long night of painting because now he was quietly snoring, his chin on his chest.

Thankfully, that sullen teenager, Tilly, arrived with their order and Sally gave Levi a gentle nudge with her elbow. She held out his triple espresso. He woke, his eyes flying open, as he looked about wondering where he was. Unfortunately, he hadn't seen the coffee Sally was holding, and he knocked the entire contents of the cup over the table. A mad scramble ensued, while daffodils, shamrocks, and Macbeth were rescued. Petronella squealed and leapt up, as hot liquid cascaded into her lap.

The coffee spread across the tabletop, and Vera pulled tissues out of her handbag. She dabbed at the puddle and the paper disintegrated immediately, leaving a pulpy, brown mess.

Everyone turned to look for Tilly, but she'd disappeared into the kitchen.

'She's ignoring the mess on purpose,' Sally said. 'I'll fetch a dishcloth.'

Seconds later, she rushed back, her eyes wide open in shock. Forgetting about the mess, Sally sat down and beckoned to the others. She leaned in, hand on her chest, fingers splayed. Everyone bent forward to listen.

'You'll never guess what I've seen!'

'What? What?'

Sally quivered with indignation. 'Look at this!' From her coat pocket, she withdrew a plastic bag filled with something red. 'It was in Beryl's bin, and they look like our hearts!' The bag was passed around and, with a nod, each person agreed.

Eyes swivelled from one face to the next. What did it mean?

'The only people in here this morning are Beryl and Tilly. But what motive could either of them have for sabotage?'

'Plenty!' Stuart's eyes lit up with anticipation. 'I think we need to interrogate them.'

Vera had a dreadful vision of a uniformed Stuart, armed with a powerful spotlight. She shook her head to banish the thought.

'With Tilly, it could be revenge,' Petronella said. 'She doesn't like us being here all the time because it gives her more work.'

'But it could be Beryl.' Stuart's eyes narrowed. 'She's charging us mates' rates; even so, we're paying her a fortune. It'd suit her if we sat here all day eating and drinking while we guard our topper. Then when we're not here, she could cause enough damage to keep us coming back. And as for the surveillance camera being broken… I bet she's just turned it off.' He stood up. 'Shall I get her—'

'No!' Vera said quickly. 'Leave it to me.' That glint in Stuart's eye was rather disturbing. They'd start with Tilly.

Vera raised her hand to summon the sulky teenager who'd re-emerged from the kitchen.

Oh, not them again! It was going to be another day of 'Tilly-get-me-this', 'Tilly-get-me-that'. Those weird, knitting people were seriously getting on her nerves.

She lingered as long as she dared by the sink and then walked over to them slowly.

Well, that was strange. It wasn't the sort of tone the old dear who was in charge usually used for ordering coffee. She was being suspiciously friendly.

'So, Tilly,' the Twinge woman said. 'What do you know about A. Godbin?'

Tilly frowned and looked up to the ceiling. A godbin? Was it some kind of new coffee? Or one of them new cakes Beryl had been experimenting with?

The Twinge woman stared intently. Her expression suggested she would not give up.

'Umm, a godbin?' Perhaps it was some sort of waste bin? Was she hinting Tilly hadn't tidied up? The table did look rather messy, but she was sure she hadn't left it like that.

'No,' Twinge Lady said slowly as if Tilly was a bit dim. 'Not a bin. A. Godbin is a person…'

This was just like school. Teachers gently prompting until they ran out of patience and then snapped.

But Tilly needed a clue. 'Is it someone from history? Only I'm not doing history at school.' Perhaps it was someone like Shakespeare or one of them kings what all had the same name.

'No.' Twinge Lady spoke slowly. 'A. Godbin is very much alive now.' She obviously still had patience left. Probably not for much longer, though.

'Like Boris Johnson?' Tilly was quite pleased with herself. She didn't know much about politics, but everyone knew about Bojo.

'Call me a stickler for convention, but I rather feel that man's name would be B. Johnson. Not A. Godbin.'

Judging by that vein throbbing in the old dear's temple and the flared nostrils, her patience had just about run out.

'Don't know, then.' Tilly shrugged. 'More coffee?'

'Triple Espresso,' said the dozy, drippy guy with the long hair and paint-stained fingers. Tilly turned away, eager to escape their strangely watchful eyes.

Work, work, work.

Tilly wondered whether to hand in her notice, but she needed the job if she was going to Torremolinos in the summer with her friend. Turning away, she rolled her eyes to the ceiling and went behind the bar to make the coffee.

When she returned, Beryl was standing next to the crazy knitting people, and apparently, she didn't know who the Godbin person was, either.

Then, the strange, little guy with glasses and wonky teeth leapt up and accused Beryl of sabotaging the weird, knitted thing they'd put on top of the post box. Twinge Lady tried to calm him down, but Beryl wasn't a woman you accused of anything. Not if you valued your life.

She came out with a few words even Tilly hadn't known, and she might have marched them all out of the café except for the dazzling flash.

Everyone stopped and turned as one, towards the man with the camera.

'Tony Parstedd. Reporter with CBN.' He flashed an identity card. 'So, what's going on here?'

'CBN?' Beryl released Stuart from a stranglehold. Sally moved away from Levi, who was now completely awake. Petronella dabbed at the coffee stain on her skirt; Stuart smoothed his comb-over back into place and rubbed his throat. Vera wondered how much money she'd have to offer the journalist to lose his photo and forget he'd been there. And it would have to be CBN... Wait! Why would a reporter from CBN be in Creaping Bottom? Unless...

‘Show me that identity card again,’ Vera demanded.

He sheepishly held it out.

Tony Parstedd, Local Reporter. Creaping Bottom News.

CBN… standing for Creaping Bottom News.

Vera began to laugh.

Flash!

A whip-round had raised seventeen pounds and thirty-four pence. Beryl had topped that up to twenty-five pounds and thrown in a box of Canberra Cupcakes, Melbourne Melts and Wagga Wagga Whirls.

Tony had deleted the two incriminating photographs from his camera, and armed with his booty, and the promise of exclusive rights to future post box toppers, he’d left the café. It had virtually been armed robbery.

The camaraderie everyone had feigned for Tony Parstedd’s benefit faltered, although outright warfare hadn’t resumed – that was in no one’s interest. There was a chilly impasse.

‘Well,’ said Vera. She was determined not to allow such disgraceful behaviour to take place again on her watch. ‘Perhaps we were hasty in accusing Beryl of sabotage.’

Beryl sniffed and peered down her nose at everyone. ‘Stabbed in the back.’

‘The evidence was rather overwhelming,’ Petronella

said, gesturing to Sally to put the bag of hearts on the table.

'Is that what Effie found on the mat this morning?' Tilly asked.

All eyes swung towards her.

She stepped backwards as if the combined force of their hostility had slammed into her chest.

Beryl's air of martyrdom slipped, to be replaced by suspicion. 'What do you know about this, Tilly Dawkins?'

'Effie said I was to tell you about it and that we have an infestation of squirrels. But she had to rush off early. Something about a blocked vacuum cleaner. Or lost bird or something.'

'So, why didn't you tell me?' Beryl's eyes bulged.

'I did. I told you Effie'd put the rubbish by the bin, and you told me to put it *in* the bin.'

'And do you know what these are?' Vera asked, thrusting the bag of hearts towards her.

Tilly shrugged, and then recognition lit her face. 'Well, I'm not sure, but they look like what Shane Fowle was waving at me last night. He might have pushed them through the letterbox.'

'And you didn't think to ask him?' Beryl's eyes were in danger of popping out.

'No, I didn't want to encourage him. He was waiting out the front for me, and he kept tapping on the window. I just ignored him, but he was holding something that looked like that.' Tilly nodded at the hearts.

'So, our masterpiece was partially dismantled by a lovesick teenager?' Vera shook her head in amazement.

'I'm surprised he didn't steal my roses,' Stuart said. 'Perhaps they were fixed too securely.'

Everyone ignored him.

Beryl crossed her arms over her chest. 'So, does that mean I'm no longer under suspicion?'

'Well…' Vera said.

'Where's the apology? And the grovelling?' Beryl tapped one toe.

'I think,' Stuart said with an edge to his voice, 'that under the circumstances we were justified—'

Vera kicked him on the shin. 'Yes, Beryl, we apologise unreservedly. We unfairly jumped to conclusions.'

'Good of you to say. I think that calls for coffee and cake all round. Added to your tab, of course.'

Stuart opened his mouth to speak but closed it again and moved his legs out of Vera's kicking range.

Once Beryl had gone to fetch coffee and a plate of her best Brisbane Brownies, Stuart shot Vera a disgruntled glance. 'The evidence against Beryl was almost overwhelming; she stood to gain financially from us. She originally offered CCTV coverage – strange it hasn't been available since we've been coming. I'm still not completely convinced…'

As if Stuart's words had summoned him, the CCTV repairman appeared from the kitchen closely followed by Beryl.

'All fixed, Beryl,' he said cheerfully. 'A software glitch. The camera was working all the time but for some reason, the footage wasn't showing up on your computer. I've tested it out, and it's fine now. It caught that fracas earlier and the bloke with the camera.'

Vera and Beryl groaned.

'Don't worry, I deleted all past footage.'

'So, there's no record?' Vera asked.

'Not on Beryl's computer, no. I've cleaned everything. But from now on, the system should work perfectly.'

Vera and Beryl sighed in unison. It appeared the incident had been contained.

The repair man left. He wondered if perhaps he should have mentioned that on some of the earlier footage he'd viewed, there were lots of squirrels running about outside the café. Beryl probably wouldn't have been interested in that. After all, they were in the street. Not Beryl's problem.

The only other thing he might have mentioned was a shifty-looking hooded character outside the café, interfering with the bobble hat on the post box. But really, why would she need to know that? Surely it was the Post Office's responsibility? And anyway, it was too late now; the footage had been deleted.

The Post Box Topper Shock

Vera Twinge rapped on the table with her spoon, calling the meeting of the Creaping Bottom Post Box Topper Society to order. There was plenty to discuss. She suspected item number one would not be popular. It was Petronella's claim for a rather pricey dry-cleaning bill to remove a coffee stain from her skirt. Oh well, best get started.

Vera was right. The comment from Stuart, the treasurer, to Petronella's request for expenses was, 'Jog on.'

That did not go down well with Petronella.

Vera stepped in to smooth over the 'pistols-at-dawn' moment. She also stepped on Stuart's foot under the table to pin him in his chair.

Vera turned to Petronella. 'I'm sorry, dear, we're sympathetic, but you might have to wait a while. We're running short of funds. It's as simple as that. We need people to join the society.'

There was a collective sigh from all five members who were gathered around their usual table in Bonzer Buns. Much hope had been placed on publicity from the local press. But that snake, Tony Parstedd, from the Creaping Bottom News, had been most unhelpful. And it had rapidly become obvious after the last edition of the newspaper that the adage 'any publicity is good publicity' was nonsense.

Yes, the dreadful reporter had come as arranged and taken a photo of them all gathered around the March post box topper with its tribute to Barbie. He'd even made a note of everyone's names, pretending he cared how they were spelt. That tiny article would probably have been buried deep within the weekly newspaper. But later, someone had stolen the Barbie doll. Coincidentally and rather conveniently, Tony Parstedd had been there to photograph the topper minus its central feature.

A photo of the damaged topper would have been embarrassing enough, but he'd put it on the front page under the headline:

VOODOO DOLL AT LARGE – Horrific Chucky-Style Doll Roams Village Causing Panic.

Since then, several people had enquired about joining their society – none of whom could knit, nor who knew what a post box topper was.

Back to square one. Although, arguably, not even as far forward as that.

Noting the pause in proceedings – or perhaps picking up on the downbeat mood in her café – Beryl arrived with slices of her special Darwin Drizzle Cake.

Stuart frowned, obviously assessing the cost, although it didn't stop him from helping himself to the largest slice.

Vera, whose appetite had been spoilt by recent press coverage, pressed on. 'So, let's get back to April.

Item two. I think we're all agreed that even though this is the month of Easter, we'll leave the religious stuff to All Saints' Church.'

Vera didn't want to fall foul of the Reverend Prendergast. She didn't privately refer to him as 'Prenderghastly' for nothing. Anything smacking of religion that wasn't owned by him was not likely to be well received.

'So, are we agreed on a display of knitted chicks, bunnies, lambs and chocolate eggs?' Vera asked.

Strangely, people seemed more interested in Beryl's Darwin Drizzle Cake, but at least no one objected. Vera ticked the item. Well, that had been easier than expected.

Next… Item three. A. Godbin. Vera had received an email complaint from him about the March topper. He'd described it – and particularly the Barbie doll in the middle – as 'abominable'.

Vera smirked. Would he run out of derogatory adjectives before she gave up planning new toppers? Oh, yes, indeed he would.

But there was nothing more than that to report about him. It was tempting to ascribe the doll-napping to A. Godbin, but in the light of recent events, Tony Parstedd had a greater motive. Or perhaps the reporter was A. Godbin? No, that was unlikely because at least A. Godbin was literate. Tony Parstedd, on the other hand…

Item number four. Security. As soon as the

Barbie doll had disappeared, there'd been a mad scramble to check the CCTV video footage. That had been a shame because, in her haste to open the laptop, Beryl had dropped it.

Ravi from Gadgets-A-Go-Go, next to Snyde the Butcher's, estimated it would take about a week to fix because he had to order an item. So, until then, there were no clues to the perpetrator of the crime. And no way of dispelling the myth of the Zombie Voodoo Doll.

Vera had noticed that maniacal look in Stuart's eyes when he'd discovered the video camera had once again failed to provide them with incriminating evidence. He was still convinced Beryl was implicated in the topper vandalism.

Now, while the CCTV system wasn't working, their only hope of keeping the next topper safe was in Levi's hands. Currently, Levi's paint-stained hands were in his lap, fluttering slightly in time with his eyelids. He was asleep again. Vera glanced at Sally, who, predictably, was sitting next to Levi and needed no more than a reassuring glance from her to stroke his sleeve lightly.

Once Levi had woken and gathered his wits, he told them about his CBPBTS Deterrent Mark II. It would be far more effective than the Mark I, which had been stuck to Barbie's feet and had therefore disappeared with her.

The prototype, Mark I, had been one of those

sound module thingamabobs that you find in audio greetings cards. You know the sort of thing… You open your birthday card, and it sings, 'Happy Birthday to you.'

Levi had acquired one such gadget in a job lot and had been so impressed, he'd wired it up so that if anyone raised Barbie, it would be activated and make a noise. It hadn't played *Happy Birthday to You*. Instead, it had blasted a few rousing bars of *The Flight of the Valkyries*. The Mark I gadget had worked so well that in a strong wind, as Barbie had leaned precariously, the tinny refrain of Wagner's most stirring stuff mysteriously wafted down the High Road.

Stuart maintained that far from being a preventative measure, that was probably what had attracted the miscreant's attention. But until Ravi fixed Beryl's laptop, and they could check the video footage, they wouldn't know who that had been.

The Mark II deterrent didn't come loaded with *Happy Birthday to You* or *The Flight of the Valkyries*. This gadget had room for a four-minute custom message. Levi explained he'd recorded a stern warning that the person who'd dared touch the topper was being videoed on CCTV. After that, he said he'd added some ghastly but creative threats about what would happen to anyone who didn't immediately replace any topper item they were tampering with. The recording concluded with the wail of a police siren to give it an air of authority.

Of course, it was hit and miss whether CCTV footage was actually being recorded, but unless the saboteur was Beryl or a society member, no one would know it might not be working. And as for the huge fine that would be imposed, well, that was an idle threat, too. But it all sounded rather official.

Levi took the Mark II deterrent and some batteries from his pocket and connected the wires.

The recording was loud.

Excruciatingly loud.

And so agonizingly long.

Had only four minutes of Vera's life ticked past? It felt like twice that. There was a stunned silence throughout Bonzer Buns when the siren howl finally whimpered and died.

Vera ticked the item off without further discussion. She wasn't sure whether it would be set off in a high wind like the Mark I. If it was, it would probably constitute a noise nuisance. The local constabulary would most likely take a dim view and be more concerned about decibels rather than the topper damage they'd already ignored.

But this was the April topper and if March had its winds, then April would have its showers. The entire gadget would most likely short-circuit if it got wet.

But what if it caught fire…? Vera's chest tightened in panic. Suppose they set the post box ablaze?

Her breath came in strangled gasps, and her

shoulders nudged her ears. With great effort, she told herself to relax. After all, she was one person, and she could only do so much. There was a plan, and she'd stick to it. Everything would be ready. During the last week, she'd been up late into the night knitting clutches of chocolate eggs, broods of chicks, flocks of sheep and an explosion of bunnies. The others were adding to the knitted pile. If something was stolen from the topper, they'd simply replace it. Not exactly satisfactory, but it would have to do.

Sally applauded when Levi had finished. 'I say, Levi. If you don't mind me saying so, I think your contraption is brilliant.'

Petronella looked impressed, too.

'I'm not sure your voice is authoritative enough on that recording,' Stuart said. 'I told you I've done Am Dram and have a powerful voice. I could have sounded much sterner than you.'

'I think Levi did it perfectly.' Sally's eyes narrowed, and Vera leaned forward to relieve her of the spoon she'd been holding. They couldn't afford to pay Beryl for bent cutlery. And if Sally had a more violent intention, then best Vera disarm her immediately.

Vera smiled at everyone. 'Thank you, Levi. Sterling job. Now, moving on. Item five.' Her shoulders slumped. Far from distracting everyone away from Stuart's abruptness, she was just about to tackle him head-on.

Four faces stared at Vera expectantly. She cleared her throat. 'Item five. Sheila Gote's complaint against a member of our society.'

Four pairs of eyes turned towards Stuart.

Yes, word had got around.

'Well, how was I to know what she was up to?' Stuart asked defensively.

Vera peered at him over the top of her glasses. 'I think the customary way is to ask. What you shouldn't have done is to perform a citizen's arrest on a woman who was posting a letter.'

'*Said* she was posting a letter. She only *said* she was posting a letter. I'm still not convinced.'

'There was no proof she was tampering with our topper. And even if she had been, I'm not sure you should have handcuffed her.'

Sally squealed in horror and held her hands to her mouth.

'And thank goodness you finally found the key,' Vera added.

'If she hadn't screamed so loudly, I wouldn't have dropped it in the first place.' Stuart scowled.

'Yes, well,' Vera said, trying to keep calm. 'What's done is done. Now, we need to decide how to make it up to Sheila. And…' she added pointedly, staring at Stuart. 'We need to decide how much we're prepared to spend out of our dwindling funds to do that.'

Stuart spluttered, but thankfully said no more.

'Perhaps Stuart might like to contribute out of his own pocket since he caused the problem.' Petronella smiled sweetly and smoothed out the dry-cleaning bill on the table in front of her.

'So,' said Beryl, appearing from nowhere. 'Did I hear someone mention gift vouchers? Only I've just started a scheme in Bonzer Buns. A twenty-five-pound voucher for a delicious afternoon tea might smooth out any misunderstandings…'

Clutching the Bonzer Buns Afternoon Tea voucher, Vera entered Debonhair Styles Salon, three doors down from Bonzer Buns. She was wearing her most ingratiating smile and was prepared to grovel. If necessary, she'd even endure a haircut. Needs must.

Sheila Gote's smile froze and slipped into something resembling a snarl when she recognised Vera.

'My dearest Sheila, on behalf of the Creaping Bottom Post Box Topper Society, I'd like to offer our abject apology for any inconvenience and embarrassment caused.' Vera smiled.

Sheila's snarl intensified.

This was going to be harder than Vera had anticipated.

'It was completely unacceptable for one of our members to carry out a citizen's arrest on you.'

'Indeed it was.' Sheila crossed her arms over her enormous chest and peered down her nose at Vera.

Oh well, there was nothing for it. Vera had hoped

it wouldn't take the Bonzer Buns voucher which she was holding in reserve. She wanted to use it to offset society expenses. But it was clear a heartfelt apology was insufficient.

'So, dearest Sheila, we wondered if you'd accept this voucher for afternoon tea at Bonzer Buns to demonstrate our regret at past… er, misunderstandings.'

With shocking rapidity, Sheila seized the envelope and tucked it in her pocket. But still, her expression was hostile. There was one more chance Vera could win the hairdresser over…

Vera kept her gaze on the pavement. She dared not catch sight of the reflection of her new hairstyle in a shop window. The breeze hadn't been as up close and personal to her neck and ears in many years. 'Chilly' didn't begin to describe the short walk from Debonhair Styles Salon back to Bonzer Buns. If only she'd brought a hat.

And woe betide anyone who laughed.

The society members were knitting furiously when Vera entered the café, although every jaw dropped as she approached their table. Silently, she sank into her seat.

Beryl arrived carrying a large Americano with soya milk, and an enormous slice of Toowoomba Tart, which she placed in front of Vera.

'That's on the house.' Beryl rocked backwards on her heels, scrutinising the new hairdo. With a tut and a sympathetic sigh, she patted Vera's shoulder, shook her head in dismay, and walked off.

Of course, it was Stuart who spoke first. 'Did you have to give Sheila the Bonzer Buns voucher?'

Always with an eye on the money, thought Vera crossly.

'Yes, I did.' She spoke through clenched teeth. 'It turns out Sheila Gote is a shrewd negotiator. And before you ask who paid for my new hairdo, I did. And if I were you, I'd stop smirking. You're booked in for an appointment in…' Vera checked her watch. 'Fifteen minutes. So, drink up.'

Stuart's hair appointment took longer than Vera's. When he arrived back in the café, he looked expectantly towards Beryl. But if he thought she was going to serve him free coffee and cake in commiseration of his new haircut, he was sadly mistaken. Beryl guffawed. She was laughing so hard she had to stagger into the kitchen to recover.

The sight of Stuart seemed to trigger one of Petronella's allergies. She held her handkerchief over her nose, periodically wiping her streaming eyes. Levi studied his knitting with head bowed, although his shoulders were shaking. Finally, he claimed he had a bout of hiccoughs and spent the next ten minutes recovering in the café's gents. Sally cleared the table and took the mugs and plates into the kitchen where she remained with Beryl.

Only Vera stared at Stuart. Well, she'd come off much better than he had. And if she didn't know any different, she'd believe the patterns Sheila had shaved in Stuart's hair spelt TWAT. But Sheila wouldn't have been that unkind, would she?

As Stuart bent to pick up his knitting, Vera saw Sheila was indeed a vindictive woman.

Then, to take Vera's mind off the cold front gathering around her ears – even in Beryl's cosy café – Ravi, from Gadgets-A-Go-Go, arrived with a parcel under his arm. Was it Beryl's laptop? If so, it was earlier than estimated. Ravi beamed as he explained he'd found a piece in stock, and that had saved him time.

Beryl set the laptop on Vera's table and raised the lid. She logged into the CCTV software and a hush fell over the group as she located the correct piece of footage.

'So, we're about to discover who the Barbie-napper is…'

Six pairs of eyes stared intently at the moving images on the screen, then blinked in unison as a popping sound came from the keyboard, followed by a plume of smoke that curled upwards. The screen went black.

Beryl yelled in frustration and snatched the computer up out of the way of Sally, who'd panicked and thrown her coffee at it to prevent a fire. Then, like a rugby player with her laptop under her arm, she ran remarkably speedily for such a large woman out of the café and along the High Road to find Ravi.

The five members of the Post Box Topper Society sat in stunned silence. Eyes moving right and left. Gazes slid from one face to the next as if trying to find some sort of sense in what they'd seen.

Finally, Stuart spoke. 'Did anyone else see the thing that…?' He raised his hands above his head, palms facing down, and lowered them slowly.

Four heads nodded vigorously, faces white with shock.

'And did anyone else see the flashing lights?'

More nods. More anxious glances.

'Has anyone got the letters U, F and O in mind?'

Sally's hand rested on her chest; fingers splayed, as if she felt the need to calm her heart. 'It was awful! That thing, flashing and hovering over the post box like that.'

Petronella found her voice. 'If it was what I think it was, this is far more sensational than a Voodoo Zombie Doll at large. It was…'

Vera finished the sentence. '…an alien abduction.'

Could it be possible? Tiny aliens had targeted Barbie and had taken her away in a miniature spaceship?

Well, it seemed each member of the Creaping Bottom Post Box Topper Society had just witnessed that…

The Post Box Topper Triumph

It was time to go home. Tilly opened the door a crack and peeped into the café. She groaned. Her boss, Beryl, was still sitting with the strange old knitting people. She'd tidied the kitchen, but before she could leave, she had to put the chairs on the tables, or in the morning, that fussy cleaner, Effie, would complain.

How much longer would they be? Tilly was getting desperate.

It wasn't even as if they were partying. They all looked miserable. Were they arguing again, like when Beryl had threatened to throttle the little guy with glasses and dodgy teeth – the one who always took the biggest bits of cake but didn't like paying up?

It didn't seem likely.

Beryl knew a lot of swear words – so many, in fact, Tilly wasn't sure if she made them up. The air would be filled with Beryl's choicest if she was arguing. No, they weren't quarrelling – in fact, they were barely talking. When someone *did* speak, the others stared in what looked like horror.

What was the matter with them?

Surely, they couldn't all be upset about the exploding laptop?

Tilly could understand Beryl being miffed. You don't expect to get your laptop fixed, only to find it blow up the first time you use it. Beryl had demanded

Ravi in Gadgets-A-Go-Go did something about it. Tilly would've liked to have been there to see that.

And to hear it.

She'd been making a list of Beryl's more colourful swear words, and she bet there'd have been a few more floating around in Gadgets-A-Go-Go.

Of course, Beryl would get her way. She always got her way. Apparently, Ravi had to order new parts and that was going to take time. He'd claimed she must have damaged it somehow because laptops didn't just blow up in the way she'd described. Beryl asked him if he'd ever worn a laptop, and once he'd worked out what she meant, he'd agreed to fix it although he'd told her she'd have to pay for some of the parts.

Beryl had not been happy. She was happy to make a profit – not so keen on paying out – as Tilly well knew. Her wages not being anything to get excited about. The Torremolinos holiday fund was growing painfully slowly.

She peered through the crack in the door again and scowled. Those old people were definitely mucking up her social life. She checked her phone.

Where RU?

RU coming?

I'm here. Where RU?

Still waitin

Wot U doin?

?????????????

Texts were flying into her phone so fast, they were almost tripping over each other.

She'd promised to visit Nan before she met her friends, so she was now seriously late. And still Beryl and the old knitters sat there, staring at each other. What was going on? Tilly put her ear to the gap in the door. The long-haired, paint-splattered bloke – the one what left coloured fingerprints on the coffee mugs – was speaking.

'But UFOs don't exist.' He didn't sound very certain.

Tilly had been about to shut the door and find some saucepans to rattle in the hope Beryl would remember she was still there. But at those words, she froze. UFOs?

Had they given up on those knitted, post box hats, and taken up something more interesting? They certainly didn't look interested. They all looked really rattled.

The dozy woman who worked in the estate agent, Crabbitt & Croppett, kept holding her hands to her mouth and squealing. And the greedy guy with dodgy teeth kept raising his hands above his head and lowering them slowly, his eyes wide and wild behind his glasses.

Tilly carried on listening. They couldn't be serious. It seemed they believed the CCTV video showed a tiny spaceship had come down in the High Road and hovered over the post box. After that, the laptop had exploded. But since the Voodoo Doll had disappeared the night the video had been recorded they'd concluded tiny aliens were responsible. The spaceship had floated over the hat-thing the knitters had stuck on top of the post box, and the aliens had somehow pulled the Voodoo Doll up into it.

Tilly wondered what they'd been drinking.

Or smoking.

She poked her nose into the gap in the door and sniffed. No tell-tale odours in there.

Her phone vibrated.

Again.

And again.

More texts. She checked the time. Five minutes had passed. Nan would be expecting her and would be worried. There was nothing for it. Tilly crept away from the door, raised a saucepan above her head and dropped it.

'Tilly!' Beryl yelled.

Tilly went to the door and looked around it innocently. 'Sorry, I just dropped something.'

'Why are you still here?' Beryl asked.

'I'm tidying up like you told me,' Tilly said virtuously.

'Well go home, I'll finish up here.'

Tilly was already out of the back door.

It wasn't far to where her nan lived.

Hurrah House.

A stupid name.

Of course, it wasn't really called that. On the big sign outside the three-storey building, it said, *The Hugo Uzzlewhit Rest and Retirement Home.* As far as Tilly could see, the first letters of those words spelt HURARH. It looked more like something a pirate might say, but spelling wasn't her strong point.

And anyway, who cared?

Whatever.

But it seemed to be close enough for the people of Creaping Bottom to refer to it as Hurrah House.

Her nan, Dora Dawkins, had been living in her retirement flat there for three years. She knew everyone and all their business. Some of the residents were more reserved than others, but Dora prided herself on being able to prise information out of the most secretive of people.

When Tilly arrived, gasping for breath, having run from the High Road, Nan was in the communal lounge. She patted the armchair next to her. 'There you are, Chickie. Where have you been? I was getting quite worried.'

Tilly told her about the ridiculous conversation she'd overheard and why she was late.

'I'd always had that Beryl Bonzer down as a sensible woman,' Nan remarked, shaking her head in disbelief. 'UFOs indeed! Just wait until I tell Mabel.'

Back in the café, the members of the society and Beryl remained seated, talking over what they'd witnessed. Their shock had given way to indecision about how to proceed.

Beryl wanted to tell everyone; keen on profiting from the crowds who'd inevitably come to the scene. Vera was more cautious. After all, if the café was inundated with UFO spotters, would they lose their table? She'd already had her fill of weird people who were interested in Voodoo. Did she really want a flood of UFO aficionados trying to infiltrate the Post Box Topper Society? And anyway, they had no proof of the alien abduction. Who'd believe them?

'It's probably just as well there's no proof,' Stuart said gloomily. 'The aliens targeted our Barbie doll. If it got out about the abduction, wouldn't people wonder how they knew about her? Aliens have got the entire universe to roam; it's a bit hard to believe they'd find their way to Creaping Bottom – and specifically, to our post box topper.'

'And your point is…?' Petronella asked.

'We might be accused of inviting them, or at least complicity in an alien operation. We might be legally liable. I'm not sure our insurance covers us for aiding and abetting an alien invasion. And what about health and safety? Who knows what sort of hygiene issues might be raised if it became known aliens had visited.'

'That's nonsense!' Sally said, but her voice was hesitant. 'Isn't it?'

No one replied.

Eventually, they agreed to keep silent on the matter and wait until Ravi had fixed the laptop so they could connect it to Beryl's CCTV camera. And in the meantime, Stuart offered to research the financial implications associated with alien abduction.

'Can't you connect Stuart's laptop to your security system, so we'd have a better idea of what we're dealing with?' Petronella asked.

'Certainly not! My laptop is my business computer. I can't go joining all sorts of unsecured networks. I have to think of my clients' security and confidentiality.'

'Whose network is unsecured?' Beryl rose, scowling, her fists bunched. Vera hastily suggested they all go home and sleep on it.

'When we get the proof, then we can decide what to do,' she suggested, hoping by that time the entire alien mess would have gone away.

'But in the meantime, we must all remain silent on the topic. Agreed?'

Everyone nodded. Even Beryl, who didn't like the sound of legal proceedings against them or the thought of placating an invasion of food inspectors.

The following day, Vera was waiting outside Bonzer Buns when it opened. She was joined shortly after by Stuart, who planned to work from the café. Petronella was at the library and Sally was at the estate agents. Levi was missing. Presumably, he'd been painting through the night and hadn't yet woken up.

Beryl let them in. They exchanged worried glances but said nothing to each other. Two women followed Vera and Stuart into the café and found a table near the window. They looked about animatedly and when Beryl greeted them and took their order, one of them said, 'So, is that where the aliens landed, just outside your café?'

Beryl dropped her pad and paper. 'Aliens?' she said weakly. 'I don't know what you mean.'

Vera appeared at Beryl's shoulder. 'Well, goodness.' Her voice was conversational. 'Aliens? Here in Creaping Bottom? How ludicrous!'

Vera exchanged glances with Beryl.

'Don't be too sure,' the woman said, tapping the table with her forefinger. 'I heard it from a friend who heard it from her friend who knows everything. And it's true. Apparently, there's even video proof. A few nights ago, aliens landed in the High Road. It seems they snatched that awful Voodoo Doll that's been terrorising the town. So, what d'you think of that?'

Vera began to laugh and, picking up on the cue, Beryl joined in.

'Oh, how funny! Really, what nonsense!' Vera said.

The woman puffed herself up. 'Well, I had it on the best authority…'

'I bet it was that rascal, Tony Parstedd from the newspaper,' Vera said. 'What a prankster. He does love a good joke.'

The two women looked disappointed.

'Oh, that's a shame. I thought it was true. It would've been quite exciting. Well, in that case, cancel the coffee and cake. There's no point staying here.'

Vera followed Beryl into the kitchen. 'How did they know? We all promised we wouldn't tell a soul.'

Beryl frowned. 'Are you sure you can trust that mongrel, Stuart? He's got shifty eyes. If I was going to put my money on anyone, it'd be him.'

'Well, it doesn't matter whoever it was who couldn't keep their mouth shut, Beryl, the story appears to be out. We now need damage control.'

Beryl's eyes narrowed. 'You know, I think we're looking at this from the wrong angle. We've got no reason to be on the defensive. We didn't invite aliens to Creaping Bottom. Surely, we can prove that? Or at least, no one can prove otherwise. I've just lost two new customers who only came because they thought we have UFOs. The story leaking out might work to our advantage.'

'I don't see how! You might be insured for such things, but the Post Box Topper Society certainly isn't.'

'Oh, lighten up, Vera. You're overreacting. You wanted publicity for your society. Well, here it is.'

'But I want people who can knit. People who

know what a post box topper is. Not a lot of conspiracy theorists.'

'Well, we're too late anyway. As you said, the story's out. If crowds of people come into Bonzer Buns to ask about the aliens, I'll make a fortune. Enough to compensate for the aggro of food inspectors, and you'll have your pick of my customers. Some of them will be able to knit, I'm sure.'

Typical. Beryl had her eye on the profit. Most likely she'd make enough to cover any legal damages. Perhaps she was the one who'd let the story out? Had Stuart been right about her all along?

The doorbell jangled.

And now, smiling broadly, Beryl rushed into the café.

It was Tony Parstedd, and he didn't look as though he wanted a cup of Beryl's finest coffee and a Brisbane Brownie.

'What are you playing at?' he demanded, an accusatory finger jabbing the air.

'And a bonzer good day to you, too,' Beryl said.

'That's a low trick! I'm in charge of headlines in Creaping Bottom. How dare you go viral! You don't get to decide what's news and what's not. What garbage! Aliens in Creaping Bottom. It's just blatant lies.'

Nevertheless, the UFO story made it to the front page, with the headline *Awful Alien April Fool's Joke Hoax.*

The report suggested the story had been invented by the Post Box Topper Society and Beryl of Bonzer Buns in a shameful attempt at self-promotion.

'How dare Tony Parstedd, of all people, accuse us of deceit,' Petronella said.

Vera had called an extraordinary meeting to discuss the UFO story and the increased interest in Bonzer Buns.

'I don't care,' said Beryl with a smug expression. 'Business has never been so good.'

'But aren't your customers all a little bit… well… intense?' Sally whispered, looking around at the occupants of the tables in the café, who were staring raptly at the post box outside the window.

'Who cares? They're fuelled by coffee and cake. I'll be able to buy a new laptop soon. Crikey, I'll be able to buy two.'

'I think you're missing the point, Beryl,' Stuart said, raising his eyebrows in a patronising way. 'What happens when the aliens don't return? People will believe we've tricked them. Imagine the backlash.'

'We can't win,' said Sally, her brows drawn together in a frown.

'Well, perhaps we can.' Levi looked up at the ceiling as he pondered. With an uncharacteristically wide-awake look, he said, 'We need to satisfy the alien sightseers, yet we also need to demonstrate we'd had no intention of tricking anyone. But also, we need to keep the rumours of the visitation alive, so Beryl fills her café, and we get preferential rates on anything we order—'

'What?' Beryl leapt to her feet. 'I never said anything about preferential rates over and above the mates' rates you're already getting!'

'But if we could keep Bonzer Buns full and our reputations intact, it would only be fair…'

Beryl chewed her lower lip and held out her hand to Levi. 'If you can do all you suggested, then I'll knock another ten per cent off your bill.'

'Twenty?' Levi put on his hopeful face.

'Done,' said Beryl.

Vera had a headache. Her heart was racing, and she wiped the cold sweat off her brow with a tissue. Then, remembering how flimsy they were, she found a hankie in her pocket and wiped all the disintegrated bits of tissue paper off her forehead. If she survived to the end of the day, then she really must buy better-quality tissues. But in the meantime, what had Levi got them into? And more importantly, how could she get them out of it?

'Twenty per cent, eh?' Stuart nodded approvingly. 'I'd have gone for twenty-five, myself.'

'Oh, shut up!' The tension was getting to Sally, too.

Petronella, Vera's right-hand woman, sat silently, her jaw slack.

No help from that quarter, then, Vera thought. The only possibility was that Levi hadn't simply been dreaming, and really did have a plan. It was vital he didn't now fall asleep, leaving them all to try to work out what it was.

Vera felt sick and to make matters worse, she'd received an email from A. Godbin that morning, calling her integrity into question over what he'd dubbed 'Aliengate'. Really! The cheek of the man!

Levi crossed his arms over his chest. 'Right, here's what we'll do. First, we deny everything…'

Vera's heart sank. For a second, she'd allowed herself to believe Levi would rescue them.

He raised a hand with paint-covered palm towards them to stop any comments. 'And then.' He smiled. 'We do this…'

It had indeed been a masterful plan. The members of the society had been invited into the local BBC radio station to talk about their post box toppers and they'd had lots of applicants wanting to join who both knew what a topper was and could actually knit. There'd been so many, Vera had made a waiting list. In fact, the society no longer needed new members because an anonymous donor had sent them a generous cheque for their 'sterling community work'. And Beryl's coffee and cake were now so cheap after all their discounts, the society's members could afford to wait a few months before they allowed anyone to join. After all, as Petronella had pointed out, they had a winning team, so why dilute it with new people who might or might not get on with the existing members?

Tony Parstedd had written a favourable article about the society and had even mentioned Bonzer Buns, to Beryl's delight. He'd praised their wit and even suggested King Charles might come to Creaping Bottom to view the Post Box Topper Society's masterpiece.

That was doubtful, but Vera could dream. Dame Vera Twinge. It had a delightful ring to it. Perhaps Tony Parstedd was after a knighthood. That was as likely as King Charles visiting the town.

But regardless of royal honours, the May topper was a masterpiece. It wasn't what Vera had planned, but, in the end, it was far better.

As soon as the date for the Coronation had been announced, the members had agreed on an appropriate topper for May, with a knitted King Charles and Queen Consort Camilla. They'd already started making crowns, union flags, coronation regalia on cushions and so on. Those pieces had all been used as planned.

However, the Creaping Bottom Post Box Society's Coronation Topper had a twist. It included guests at the coronation. But not just any guests. Not bishops, lords and ladies. No, Levi had proposed they create a scene that imagined what the Coronation might look like, had the King invited beings from a neighbouring planet. Not so much alien *invasion* as alien *invitation.*

The knitted spaceship had been sprayed silver, and Levi had attached eight fine, strong wires to the bottom. It looked rather like a metallic spider standing up on its legs and gave arachnophobe, Sally, quite a turn. However, once each wire had been covered in a yellow knitted tube, it looked just like a hovering spacecraft that was projecting light beams from its underside onto the earth below. A knitted ladder dangled from beneath the spaceship down which green-knitted aliens climbed to the Coronation scene at its base.

The rumours about real aliens had been explained by claiming the Post Box Topper Society had been planning their knitted alien coronation and the story had somehow leaked out. As so often happens, the facts had become distorted until people had come to believe Creaping Bottom had really been visited by aliens.

Exactly what would happen if aliens really did visit the town again, Vera had no idea. But really, what were the chances?

A. Godbin had predictably been incensed at the May post box topper and had emailed to tell Vera so. But she was confident that he was mistaken, and that King Charles wouldn't see their interpretation of their imaginative Coronation as treason. That was simply ridiculous.

Roll on, next month, Vera thought. They'd survived May. What would June bring?

The Post Box Topper Photo-Opportunity

Brainstorming.

Well, not so much brainstorming, as *brain-draining,* Vera thought. Petronella had suggested holding the session so they could decide on a design for June's post box topper display.

The alien coronation topper they'd created for May would be hard to beat, and many eyes would be upon them. Petronella was now poised with a felt tip pen over the large piece of paper laid on their usual table in Bonzer Buns. Much of it was covered in words and arrows, but little of it would be any use.

Stuart puffed himself up to his most pompous. 'Well, obviously, we'll have lots of flowers, and since my roses were so successful in the February Valentine's Day Topper, I'll volunteer to knit some more.'

Vera's sharp eyes intercepted the dismayed gazes between Petronella, Levi and Sally. Stuart's knitted creations had borne as much similarity to delicate velvet roses, as frayed, tarry rope did to silk thread. But thankfully, no one had pointed that out – so far. Vera thought it was probably only a matter of time…

'Flowers? No,' said Levi firmly. 'That's too predictable.'

'But nothing says *June* like summer flowers,' Stuart protested.

'How about saying *June* in poetry?' Sally asked.

Stuart scoffed, 'You mean like the moon in June? The only other things I can think of to rhyme with June are spoon and croon.'

'Well, recently I've been trying my hand at poetry,' said Sally. 'And I think it can be done.'

Vera barely suppressed a groan. She suspected Sally had been writing love poems and her fears were confirmed when Sally gazed lovingly at Levi and pointed out his name didn't rhyme with anything. Thankfully, if he'd noticed, he said nothing.

Am I getting too old for this? Vera wondered. Her position as chairperson of the Creaping Bottom Post Box Topper Society was becoming harder to maintain. There was so much to think about, especially since the May topper had been featured in the national press. Stuart was becoming increasingly difficult to control. She was growing weary. Perhaps one more month and then she'd resign?

'June, soon, moon, spoon, croon.' Petronella wrote the words on her brainstorming paper.

Stuart wore his most patronising expression. 'Are you suggesting we knit a moon and a spoon? I suppose someone with a lot of experience like me might manage that, but how do you propose we represent *croon*?'

'Where there's a will…' said Levi.

'Let's move on,' Vera said, hoping to steer the conversation away from Sally's poetry, as well as from random objects that rhymed with June.

There was silence for a few moments as everyone pursued their own thoughts.

'Tune?' suggested Levi.

'How do you knit a tune?' Stuart asked.

'I was just saying tune rhymes with June.'

More silence.

Beryl approached the table. 'More coffee, anyone?'

Well, thank goodness for that, thought Vera. By the time everyone had ordered coffee and Darwin Dream Puffs – Beryl's Cake of the Day – all thoughts of moons, spoons, and crooning tunes would be forgotten.

Beryl brought their order and as she placed the last mug on the table, she said, 'Prune. And balloon. Oh, and baboon.'

Vera decided enough was enough.

'Well, since this is only a brainstorming session, let's not get carried away along one avenue of possibility. Would someone care to come up with something else that screams *June*, but doesn't rhyme with it?'

'Weddings,' said Sally with a gaze from beneath her lashes at Levi. 'June is the month for weddings.'

Like a tyre with a puncture, Vera felt her enthusiasm – and her will to live – escape in a *whoosh.* This was turning into Sally's veiled declaration of love to Levi. Surely Petronella, the practical one, would steer them back towards sense.

'I think that's a marvellous idea,' Petronella said. 'We could knit all the figures in a wedding ceremony.'

'With lots of summer flowers like roses,' Stuart added, his eyes alight with excitement.

Even Levi nodded his approval.

Vera considered bringing forward her resignation as chairperson. She'd almost lost control of the meeting again. Surely, it was time for her to go? On the other hand, the more she thought about it, the more Sally had a point. June was a month for weddings. And perhaps, with a little imagination, she could rein in Sally's overexuberance.

No, she wasn't ready to relinquish her grasp of the society. And realistically what else would she do with her time if she resigned her chairpersonship? As soon as A. Godbin learnt she'd moved on, he'd divert his complaining emails to whoever took over. With surprise, Vera realised she'd miss them. They made her hackles rise, but they gave her a reason to get up in the morning with the determination to carry on.

'But it can't be just any old wedding,' Petronella said. 'Remember, the eyes of the world are upon us after our alien coronation topper. We need something with just as much *je ne sais quoi*. And even more *pzazz*.'

Vera's voice came out in a squeak. 'You're not suggesting an alien wedding, are you? Or a wedding between an alien and a human?' That would throw up all sorts of moral issues. What would Reverend Prendergast say?

'No,' said Petronella. 'Definitely not. I'd rather forget about aliens. What I mean is we need an extra ingredient that nobody else has thought of.'

Four pairs of eyes stared at her blankly.

How could they come up with something nobody had ever thought of? Gradually, everyone's gaze slid towards Levi, who was now staring at the ceiling as if receiving a message from above.

Well, he was the creative one. If anyone could know *quoi* and come up with an idea that nobody else could think of, it would be Levi.

'How about something that would ensure people wanted to have their photograph taken next to our topper?' he said finally.

'Such as?' Vera was disappointed. People already did selfies by their post box toppers. She'd hoped for something more pzazzy than that.

With a faraway look in his eyes, Levi added, 'I was thinking we could knit a bride and a groom—'

'Well, obviously,' Stuart said snippily. 'How can you have a wedding without a bride and groom?'

'No, wait!' Levi stretched out one arm, his finger pointing as if he could see a vision. 'What I mean is an almost life-size bride and groom – well, post-box-sized, anyway.'

Vera had bought into his vision so completely that on hearing such stupidity, she once again felt like a deflated tyre. 'We can't possibly have anything so large on top of a post box. The wind will simply blow it over.'

‘Not 3-D stuffed figures on top of the post box. I meant 2-D, knitted bride and groom panels dangling down either side. What we’d do is attach their heads to the topper bonnet and let them hang down. We’ll attach some weights on their feet, so they won’t blow about. Passers-by can link arms with the knitted figure and have their photos taken.

‘I think that’s a bonzer idea,’ said Beryl, who’d crept up to listen. ‘That would certainly bring the crowds.’ Her eyes lit up at the prospect of all those thirsty, hungry potential customers in her café.

The more Vera thought about it, the more Levi’s idea appealed.

‘Well done, Levi, I think your idea has legs,’ said witty Petronella.

Everyone laughed except Stuart. ‘Well, of course they’ll have legs. You can’t have a legless bride and groom. But d’you think we’ll be allowed to attach anything to the side of the post box?’

‘Well, we’re not blocking the aperture, so I don’t see why not. And I can always check with the postmistress first,’ Petronella said.

Tilly pushed open the door to the café, her usual bored expression replaced by a look of astonishment.

‘You’re late,’ Beryl growled. ‘I don’t pay you to bludge.’

‘I’ve just been at Hurrah House seeing Nan and you’ll never guess what…’

'I don't pay you to keep me guessing, either,' Beryl said. 'There are tables to clean.'

'There was nearly a punch-up between your cleaner, Effie, and one of the old dears,' Tilly blurted out.

That caught Beryl's attention. 'Fair dinkum?'

'Yeah. It was Effie and the weird old bag who lives next to my nan. They almost ended up in a fight. Apparently, Effie snuck into her flat to empty the bin. You know how she can't keep her hands off rubbish. And the old bag, who'd been down to check the post, came back and found her. You should have heard the language…'

Ten minutes later, during which time Levi had drawn several sketches of the knitted bride and groom panels that would dangle from the topper's bonnet, Effie entered the café.

She was quivering. Her face contorted with rage.

'I've never been so insulted in my life,' she said, one sausage-fingered hand against her chest. 'I think I'll have an oat milk latte with honey and two shots of caramel syrup, please Beryl. I need something to calm myself down. That Alice woman is the rudest person I've ever met. I was trying to do her a favour. And she turned on me.

'She's just a weirdo,' Tilly said in an unfamiliar show of solidarity with Effie. 'I shouldn't take no notice. My nan says she's a right old misery. Never joins in with anyone. And if someone knocks at her door, she won't open it. She talks to them through the crack. I reckon she's got dead bodies hidden in there.'

'That wouldn't surprise me at all.' Effie sniffed with the air of a martyr. 'It didn't smell too good in there either, which is why I wanted to clear out her bin for her. My brother, Des, who's in the flat on the other side of her, says she might be quiet when she's in the lounge with everyone else, but when she's in her flat, she's really noisy. Tapping and whirring. He thinks she chops up fruit and puts the bits in one of them blenders what you make smoothies in. A health nut. I wouldn't be surprised if he was right. She's stronger than she looks – she had my arm up behind my back before I knew it and frogmarched me out of her flat.'

'I bet she's a secret mass murderer,' Tilly said. 'She probably chops up the bodies and then puts the bits in the—'

'That's enough!' Beryl said. 'This is a respectable establishment we don't need to talk about…' she mouthed, *dead bodies.* 'I'm sure you've got tables to clear, Tilly. And, Effie, I'll get you a double espresso with oat milk and all the trimmings. And a Darwin Dream Puff. And if you stop talking about…' She mouthed, *dead bodies*, 'I'll bring you two puffs.'

Despite the inauspicious start of the brainstorming session, everyone agreed the June wedding-themed topper was a huge success. Even the Reverend Prendergast had stopped Vera in Snyde's Butcher's and complimented her on the display. It appeared to have prompted several couples to book their ceremonies at All Saints' Church.

Thankfully, as far as Vera was concerned, Levi and Sally had not been one of those couples. Not that Vera wanted to keep them apart, but their relationship – such as it was – could be thought of as very one-sided, and eventually, Sally was bound to be disappointed. Levi lived for his art, and Vera was certain it would never have worked out.

Once again, tourists had begun to arrive in Creaping Bottom to have a photograph taken next to the post box. Men and women queued up to link arms with either the bride panel on one side of the post box, or the groom panel on the other.

Although the postmistress, Miss Witter, had initially given her permission, she later claimed she hadn't understood exactly what would be involved. She was often to be found outside the Post Office with hands planted on hips, frowning at the queue next to her post box. But nobody else had complained.

Well, that wasn't quite true. Of course, A. Godbin had sent Vera an angry email. She grinned at the thought. He'd accused the June post box topper of being sacrilegious and had told her he intended to inform the Archbishop of Canterbury who'd personally put a stop to the nonsense.

Vera had laughed out loud. She assumed the archbishop had more important things on his mind.

And anyway, unknown to A. Godbin, the Reverend Prendergast, one of the archbishop's minions, had already praised her for extolling the virtues of marriage.

Vera wasn't sure the topper was such a wonderful example for marriage, anyway. It appeared to be more of an excuse for putting a photo on the Instagram – whatever that was. Tilly had explained, but it still made no sense to Vera. Tilly also stressed photos must be accompanied by some sort of hashtag code – #CreapingBottomWedding. Vera took her word for it. She had no idea what, nor where the Instagram was. Neither did she know what trending meant. But Tilly had been impressed and had even posed next to the groom. She'd wrapped his knitted arm around hers and, with the silly pout she assumed when she took a selfie, she'd snapped herself.

The month of June also saw a bizarre alliance form between Tilly and Effie. They'd joined forces, both firmly believing that Alice, the woman who lived between Effie's brother, Des, and Tilly's Nan, Dora, was a mass murderer. They were taking it in turns to keep her under surveillance.

When Vera pointed out, there had been no murders in the area, for as long as she could remember, the unlikely pair of sleuths were forced to reconsider. The following day, a dog went missing, and they suggested

Alice was the culprit. After all, they pointed out, how many pets went missing each week? She could be responsible for all of them.

Privately, Vera didn't think many pets went missing at all. Certainly not enough to feed the blender that both Des and Dora could hear whirring away into the night, as well as the tapping and chopping.

But so long as Effie and Tilly were on friendly terms, Beryl was reasonably content – and as for Vera, she didn't care. She had problems of her own. The bride and groom knitted panels were proving so popular they'd become rather tatty.

The members of the society had already replaced both figures twice and there were still another few days of June left.

Would they last until the July topper was ready? It was looking unlikely. And what's more, the wedding ceremony taking place on the top had been disturbed too. Not vandalised, exactly – just disturbed. The figures hadn't been removed, but they were somewhat... well... crushed. Why somebody would squash their post box topper figures wasn't clear. And there had been rubbish on the topper too. Bits of vegetation too heavy to have blown up there, so somebody must've deliberately dumped it on top. It was very disappointing that someone could be so spiteful.

Each morning Vera arrived in Creaping Bottom High Road with a dustpan and brush. She carefully plumped up the knitted figures in the wedding ceremony on the top and brushed away the debris.

But at last, some good news. Ravi from Gadgets-A-Go-Go promised Beryl her laptop would be ready by the last Thursday in June. The technician would then return to ensure the CCTV camera worked and recorded footage.

By Friday morning, Vera would know who the culprit was. Assuming Beryl's laptop didn't blow up again, of course. Vera controlled her urge to skip as she made her way, handbag over her arm, and dustpan and brush in her hand, towards the post box. She would soon know the identity of A. Godbin.

On Friday morning, Sally, Petronella, Stuart, Levi and Vera sat around the laptop in Bonzer Buns, holding their breath as Beryl located the CCTV software and rewound the footage.

That morning there'd been a hole in the bride panel, as if someone had slashed it with something sharp. The groom had also been torn and there'd been quite a lot of rubbish, as if someone had picked up a handful of leaves and other litter and thrown it on the top of the post box.

Could A. Godbin have been so petty? Honestly, what was wrong with the man?

All eyes were on Beryl's screen.

So far, so good. The laptop whirred gently and

although Vera sniffed, afraid of detecting the smell of hot plastic or metal, it appeared to be working perfectly.

'Here,' said Beryl, stopping the video and pressing play. They all leaned in, their heads side by side. Vera noted Sally had sat next to Levi and leaned her head against his, but Vera wasn't concerned. Everyone's undivided attention was on the laptop screen. They watched in silence as the perpetrators… yes, not one, but several – damaged their June post box topper display. When all had become clear, they leaned back in their seats.

'Well,' Vera said finally. 'I wasn't expecting that.'

Her words prompted everyone to speak at once. Beryl went to fetch coffee and slices of Adelaide Angel Cake.

Vera sighed. She'd been so certain she'd uncover the identity of A. Godbin. On the other hand – and quite perversely – she wondered whether it was a good thing he hadn't been involved. She still had that mystery to solve.

And solve it she would.

But in the meantime, the vandals of the June topper had been uncovered.

Squirrels.

They'd used the two knitted panels as ladders and had scrambled to the top, to sit up there eating nuts and doing whatever squirrels do in the middle of the night.

Vera began to laugh, and the others joined in. Well, there were only a few more days left in June and then they'd replace the wedding scene with the July topper. And A. Godbin was still out there, possibly poised to send her another aggravating email. One day, she'd have the satisfaction of tracking him down and exposing him.

Vera raised a toast with her coffee to the Creaping Bottom Post Box Society. The others echoed her words.

Oh yes, Vera thought to herself, *as aggravating as the post of chairperson is, I love every minute.*

The Post Box Topper Summer Scene

Bonzer Buns had become the meeting place for not only the Creaping Bottom Post Box Topper Society but for what Vera had begun to think of as the Tilly and Effie Private Investigation Bureau. Not that the pair of would-be sleuths had any clients. However, they'd taken it upon themselves to keep the woman they suspected of being a serial killer under surveillance.

Tilly's grandmother Dora, and Effie's brother, Des, lived on either side of the murder suspect, Alice, and they'd joined with Tilly and Effie to keep an eye – and an ear on her.

Vera thought it was a lot of nonsense. Alice Gruber might be a grumpy old woman who made strange noises during the night, but bad temper and nocturnal wanderings weren't criminal offences as far as Vera knew. But then, she actually didn't want to know. She'd seen Alice in the village but had never spoken to her. Neither did she want to. The woman had a sour face.

And Vera had problems of her own. The July topper. How would it be received? She was waiting at the CBPBTS table to discuss it with the other members who, incidentally, were late. Vera beat an angry rhythm on the tabletop with her fingers.

Meanwhile, Tilly and Effie at the TAEPIB table looked at each other forlornly.

'Doesn't that woman ever sleep?' Tilly grumbled.

'She made those tapping and whirring noises into the early hours. I don't think I'll be able to keep this surveillance up much longer. I've got school on Monday. I'm already in trouble for nodding off in geography.'

'I shouldn't worry,' said Effie smugly. 'I think there was an accident last night and when I saw Alice in the communal sitting room this morning, her black eye appears to bear that out. It might put a stop to her shenanigans.'

'Oh, I wondered what the crash and yelp was all about.'

Effie had sat for hours with her ear against a glass which she'd pressed to the dividing wall between Des's and Alice's apartments. She suspected Tilly, who was staying with her gran on the other side of Alice's rooms, had spent most of her time listening to that racket she called music through her AirPods. But no one could have missed the bang. Effie had run next door and knocked on the pretext of making sure Alice was all right, but no one had answered.

At least while Alice was at home, she wasn't murdering anyone. Although from the metallic banging, Effie wondered if she wasn't constructing some sort of mantrap.

When Beryl came out of the kitchen, she eyed her two employees suspiciously, then glanced about the café, presumably looking for something that hadn't been done.

Finding nothing, she frowned at them. 'I don't know what this unholy alliance signifies, but I hope you're going to behave with a bit more sense than you did yesterday, Tilly.'

Effie and Tilly looked at each other sympathetically. 'Never mind, dear,' said Effie, patting Tilly's hand. 'Everyone will be grateful when we've stopped Creaping Bottom's serial killer in her tracks.'

Fed up waiting for the others, Vera had gone outside to survey the July's post box topper that she and the others had fitted the previous evening. She'd had several sleepless nights during the planning phase. It was becoming harder to think of something original and eye-catching.

The May Alien Coronation scene had been a media sensation. Then, the June Wedding spectacle with its post box-sized knitted panels of the bride and groom, had been photographed by people from far and wide. Unfortunately, although the shopkeepers of Creaping Bottom had rejoiced at the influx of tourists, it had also caused problems. Miss Witter, the postmistress, had repeatedly lost her temper because of the crowds queueing to have their photographs taken with the knitted bride or groom on the post box.

'Too much noise,' she'd said to anyone who'd listen. 'Too much traffic and pavement congestion. Too many tourists.'

Unfortunately, she'd been very vocal, and those waiting in the queue to have their photo taken with the bride or groom had started taking photographs of Miss Witter and posting them on social media.

Vera was still rather hazy about exactly what or where the X that had once been Twitter was, but it obviously wasn't a good thing when it was associated with the hashtag #BitterWitterTwitterX. She suspected Tilly had been involved, because how else would the tourists and sightseers have known the postmistress's name?

Vera patted the edge of the grass-green crocheted bonnet with the blue 'lake' in the middle that sat on the top of the post box. Well, that was July's topper, for better or worse. During the planning stages, she'd rejected several outlandish plans from Levi who'd been in favour of courting the world's media attention.

'We can't keep this pace up,' Vera had complained and, eventually, everyone had agreed. How could they outdo the previous two months' toppers? And if it had been possible, how would they be able to keep it up?

That hadn't been the only problem. Their success had prompted many of the village's shopkeepers and major players to – first, suggest they were featured in a post box topper – and later, to beg.

Ravi from Gadgets A-Go-Go had Vera shaking her head in disbelief when he'd proposed they knit the interior of his workshop, with a woollen Ravi sitting inside as an advertisement for his business. Some people obviously believed in miracles.

Sheila Gote had suggested they featured the Debonhair Styles Salon to publicise it. She'd reminded Vera of how stressed and humiliated she'd been when Stuart had put her under citizen's arrest. That had merely reminded Vera of how stressful and humiliating it had been when Sheila had given her a 'Revenge Haircut'. No, the woman had already had her pound of flesh.

Miss Witter, the postmistress, had demanded compensation for the aggravation of the squirrels invading the top of her post box and the insulting crowd who Vera and her 'cronies' had incited to riot outside her Post Office. She'd insisted she should be featured on the July topper. After all, weren't they using *her* post box? What about wear and tear? If Miss Witter had been nicer and had said 'please,' Vera might have considered it, but under the circumstances…

Mr Snyde, the butcher, had also requested Vera promote his shop, and he'd been most aggrieved when she'd turned down his bribe of six extra sausages.

And even Prenderghastly – the Reverend Prendergast – had floated the idea that, since the church fete would take place in July, she might like to feature All Saints'. Perhaps him preaching on his pulpit…?

And, to top it all, that wretched reporter, Tony Parstedd had threatened that if she didn't do a topper with a newspaper theme, starring him, he couldn't be held responsible for the outcome.

With each person, Vera had been polite but firm. The answer had been 'no'. The Creaping Bottom Post Box Topper Society would neither be bullied nor bought. There would be no advertising.

The other members agreed with her. If she favoured one person, the other villagers would plague Vera until the society's toppers had advertised every business in Creaping Bottom. How dull would that be? And Vera would not bring Post Box Topperism into disrepute by having it linked with corruption. She'd stand firm. She refused to be moved. She would not allow it. She would—

'All right! We've got the point, Vera,' Stuart had said testily. 'Please could you stop lecturing us.'

So, that was that. They'd decided on a simple summer display with knitted people enjoying the park – picnicking and playing summer sports. Levi had suggested cyclists but eventually, he'd given up knitting bicycles and had made little models out of wire around which he wound wool.

Stuart said he was cheating, but Vera thought they looked rather cute with the knitted riders on top in lurid colours to represent their Lycra outfits.

Everyone had worked very hard and now Vera admired the result. A woman rowed a boat across the blue crocheted lake next to a lone swimmer, and nearby, a fisherman sat with his rod. On the green crocheted grass, hikers hiked, sunbathers sunbathed, dog walkers walked dogs and cricketers played cricket.

Yes, it was a thoroughly summery scene. It might not draw tourists but perhaps that was a good thing…

Beryl woke in the early hours. Her dreams had been of Effie and Tilly's Creaping Bottom serial killer, who compounded her wrongdoings by thumping and whirring at night.

Whirring.

It must have been the noise that had prompted Beryl's strange dreams.

Whirring? What could possibly be whirring at 2.25 am?

Beryl's eyes were drawn to the windows. Bright lights blazed outside her curtains. That definitely wasn't normal.

With a sigh, she got up and peeped out. Sleep was instantly banished as she stared in disbelief. The tiny aliens in their spacecraft had returned. They hovered over the post box with lights playing down on the topper, operating something that looked remarkably like a pair of scissors suspended beneath the spaceship.

Beryl had had enough. There were plenty of villages in this country and plenty of post box toppers. Let those aliens find another one to pester. She wanted her sleep.

Tugging on her dressing gown and thrusting her feet into slippers, she stomped downstairs to the cleaning cupboard. She seized a broom and, after quietly letting herself out of the café, raised her weapon to shoulder height and swung. The blow sent the alien spaceship hurtling as far as Mr Snyde's butcher's shop, where it plummeted to earth, finally coming to rest next to the bus stop.

The following morning, Vera, Stuart, Levi, Sally and Petronella gathered around their usual table in the café.

'And this,' said Beryl triumphantly, waving a carrier bag aloft, 'is the alien spaceship.'

She pulled out a drone and placed it on the table. Everyone stared silently, shaking their heads in disbelief.

Vera didn't know whether to be pleased there didn't appear to be an alien invasion or annoyed she'd been taken in by a drone.

'I watched it hover over the topper. It had downlighters and a sort of snipper tool suspended beneath, which was trying to chomp at the knitted figures,' Beryl said.

'A drone.' Stuart leaned forward to pick up the battered item. 'Who'd have thought it? But it is fiendishly clever.'

Vera beat him to it and pulled it out of his reach. Stuart could be remarkably clumsy sometimes.

'Is there any way we can trace the owner?' Petronella asked.

'We probably won't be able to tell that unless we can mend it. I'd be happy to give it a go. I'm a demon with a screwdriver.' Stuart reached out for it again, but Vera pretended not to see and kept firm hold of it.

A demon with a screwdriver? Well, that was true. Stuart was a demon with any sort of tool.

'Let's take it along to Ravi,' Beryl said.

'Ahhh.' The sound came from Vera's lips like air from a slow puncture in a tyre. 'Sadly, we may have burned our bridges with Ravi. He wanted us to advertise his shop on our topper and I refused. Things got rather heated.'

'There's no need to bother Ravi. I'd be happy to take it home and tinker.' Stuart reached out for the drone yet again, but Vera held on to it, looking about desperately to the others for help. She knew they understood her dilemma.

'Perhaps—' Levi said.

'Yes?' Petronella, Sally and Vera said simultaneously.

Levi jumped with surprise at the hasty and enthusiastic response, then continued, 'Perhaps I might have an idea.'

'Thank goodness for that,' muttered Vera under her breath. She handed him the drone.

Sally batted her eyelashes. 'Oh, Levi, you're so clever.'

'Well, that remains to be seen,' said Stuart, glowering at everyone.

Levi held the drone away from Stuart. 'What we

must do is knit a new figure dressed in a white lab coat, like the one Ravi wears at work. Then someone needs to make a tiny laptop—'

'Knit a laptop?' Petronella asked.

'No, make one out of wood and paint it. I think Stuart would be good at that.'

Stuart? Vera thought. What is Levi saying? Stuart was probably the one the least likely to make a success of such a tiny object. On the other hand, Stuart was now beaming. She'd obviously underestimated Levi's people-management skills.

Levi continued, 'We'll place the new figure and the laptop next to the picknickers and tell Ravi he's part of our topper but that unfortunately we can't include advertising of any description.'

'But advertising was what he wanted,' said Petronella.

'I know, but we'll make it clear it's that or nothing. The honour of appearing on our topper, might compensate…'

'It makes sense,' said Petronella. 'However, what will happen when the others who've badgered us to advertise them find out Ravi has been featured on July's topper?'

'Well, I have another idea,' said Levi.

It had meant a lot of hard work that night, altering the characters that were already on the topper and also getting new figures ready.

A dog collar was an easy addition to the fisherman, who was to be passed off as the Reverend Prendergast.

Only small alterations were needed for the two picknickers. A knitted sausage was placed in the hand of the male to convert him into Mr Snyde, and an elaborate woollen hairstyle was added to the woman, to turn her into Sheila Gote. The knitted version of Ravi in his white lab coat sat on the blanket with them, his laptop on his lap. Thankfully, Stuart had made a good job of the computer, much to everyone's surprise.

A sack of post was added to the rowing boat, to turn the rower into Miss Witter delivering mail.

'Oh no! We've forgotten Tony Parstedd,' Petronella said as the last figure was placed back on the topper.

'Tony Parstedd? No, don't worry, he's on there,' said Levi.

'The dog walker?'

Levi shook his head.

'The cyclist? Tennis player?'

Levi smiled and pointed at a small triangular knitted shape behind the swimmer and next to the rowing boat.

'Ah!' said Petronella. 'Shark's dorsal fin?'

Luckily, Ravi was thrilled with his woollen picknicking avatar and had been intrigued when he'd learnt about the drone. He'd offered to look at it. A day later, he announced he'd fixed it and using a bit of technical wizardry, he hoped it would automatically fly home when he switched it on.

Beryl and the members of the Creaping Bottom Post Box Society gathered outside Gadgets-A-Go-Go for the grand switching on ceremony. Everyone wore trainers, or at least shoes they might easily run in. If the drone took off – although that was rather doubtful – everyone would need to pursue it, or at least keep it within sight until its destination was revealed.

Vera's heart was already pounding, and the chase hadn't yet begun. Would this be the occasion when she came face to face with A. Godbin? She had a tremulous feeling in her stomach that said it was.

'Ready?' asked Ravi.

Everyone lined up as if starting a race. Six heads nodded.

'Go!' shouted Ravi as he switched it on and the drone rose vertically. It hovered for a few seconds above them.

For an instant, Vera wondered if it was going to keep going up. Had they been wrong? Was it really an alien spaceship? But, after rotating through one hundred and eighty degrees, the drone shot off along the High Road, about six feet above their heads.

'Run!' yelled Vera. 'Follow that drone!'

At the post-chase meeting in Bonzer Buns, Ravi was included in the commiserations. Having spent so much time mending the drone, he'd felt he had a vested interest and had joined in the race to discover the owner. He, Levi and Sally had been the fastest and had pursued the flying object as it turned off the High Road and headed towards Hurrah House. Then, just as they'd thought that was its destination, it had veered away and set off in the opposite direction towards Upper Chortle. About half a mile along the road, the drone had coughed and spluttered. Finally, it had divebombed and crashed.

'I was so sure it was heading for Hurrah House,' Levi said, his face wrinkled in a frown.

'That's full of old people,' said Stuart. 'The owner of the drone is hardly likely to have been one of them.'

'Are you saying all old people are nice?' Vera's voice was cutting. 'Or are we just too stupid?'

'More coffee anyone?' said Beryl soothingly. 'I've got some slices of Perth Pistachio Pie just out of the oven…'

Beryl might well have renamed the cake Perth Peace Pie because the slices were so large and delicious no one had the heart to argue.

Vera mused as she munched. It was disappointing they hadn't unearthed A. Godbin.

But his time would come. She was certain. And in the meantime, there was still plenty more Perth Pistachio Pie. And of course, they still had to discuss the planning of the August topper…

The Post Box Topper Animal Extravaganza

Vera had expected everyone to ignore the July post box topper. A pretty summer scene with its dog walkers, fisherman and picnickers should not have provoked as much interest as it had. But everyone in Creaping Bottom had wanted to know who each knitted figure was supposed to be and to guess who the few unidentified characters were.

Ravi, Sheila, Mr Snyde, Prenderghastly and Miss Witter had proudly told anyone who'd listen which figures represented them. Of course, Tony Parstedd hadn't spotted the triangular fin on the knitted pond surface nor realised that the imagined shark below it was supposed to be him. Believing he'd been deliberately snubbed, he'd vowed revenge.

As for the unidentified figures, Vera knew they hadn't been based on anyone. However, no one had believed her, so in the end, when asked, she'd merely shrugged, and with an inscrutable look on her face, had said she was unable to divulge that information.

So, claims for the two unidentified cyclists and the dog walker were many and varied. Conversations had become heated as people insisted they'd been the inspiration for each of the figures.

One lunchtime, when Vera, Petronella, Stuart, Levi and Sally were in Bonzer Buns, a fight broke out by the post box. Two men with dogs on leads had come to blows after one of them had claimed he and his canine friend had been the inspiration for the dog and its owner.

Levi rushed outside, ready to defend the topper because it looked as though the knitted dog walker was about to be poked into oblivion as each human dog walker pointed out features that proved it resembled him, and of course, his dog.

'That is a cockapoo,' the chunky, ginger-haired man said, poking the knitted dog. 'Just like my Nutkins.'

'Nonsense,' said the blond-haired, bearded man, jabbing the knitted dog with his finger. 'Everyone can see it's a Labradoodle like my William the Conqueror.'

Levi stepped between them and held up his hand. 'Excuse me please, gentlemen. I'm sorry to disappoint you both, but I knitted that dog-walking avatar, and I based it on myself.'

Well done, Levi, Vera thought. *Very creative.* She'd followed the others out into the street. It wasn't true, but it had put paid to the dispute.

Or perhaps it hadn't.

Chunky squared up to Levi. 'It looks nothing like you. And what's more, you haven't even got a dog.'

Levi's mouth opened and closed. Opened and closed.

But sadly, not creative enough, thought Vera.

Then Sally stepped forward. 'I think the little

knitted chap looks exactly like Levi. Handsome and suave. And as for his dog, it's currently in the canine beauty parlour.'

Well done, Sally, Vera thought.

But Chunky wasn't about to give up. 'And what sort of dog is it? A Labradoodle or a Cockapoo?'

Sally stared at Levi.

Levi stared at Sally.

'A cocka—' said Sally.

'A labra—' said Levi at the same time.

'That is,' said Levi, 'it's a Cocka-Loodle-Doo.'

There was silence for a few moments while each dog walker looked down at his own dog.

Finally, Chunky said, 'Well, where do Nutkins and I have to apply to be knitted?'

'I'll take your names,' said Sally, stepping forward. 'But I have to warn you there's a long waiting list, so we may not get around to you until 2025 at the earliest.'

Both men gave their names and contact details and walked away in opposite directions.

'You were magnificent, Sally,' said Levi.

'And you were useless, Levi,' said Sally. 'I mean, Cocka-Loodle-Doo?'

She and Levi collapsed in giggles.

Well, thought Vera, *they seem to be getting on well together.* Perhaps they might be at a turning point in their relationship.

Brought together by a knitted dog walker and a

hitherto unknown crossbreed of dog. Or possibly crossbreed of species.

Not the strangest thing that Vera had seen during her tenure of the Post Box Topper Society chairpersonship.

They went back into Bonzer Buns to celebrate Sally's triumph and to consider the August topper.

Stuart suggested flowers, and everyone groaned.

'What, what? It's summer. Flowers grow in summer.' Stuart scowled at them. 'What have you lot got against flowers? It's probably illegal to be so flowerphobic.'

Everyone ignored him.

Sally looked up the special days in August on her phone, and read out, 'Women's World Cup Day…'

'No,' said Petronella. 'I loathe football.'

'How about Sea Serpent Day?' asked Sally. She looked up to gauge everyone's reaction, but everyone stared at her blankly.

'Sea Serpent Day doesn't appeal? Well, we also have various international days. What about the International Day for Owl Awareness, or for cats, dogs, orangutans or youths – presumably human youths? And not just international *days*, we have International Bat Night. Then there are World Days for lions, elephants and lizards… Is that enough?'

'They're all heavily biased towards the animal kingdom,' said Vera. 'Is there anything that's not animal-related?'

Sally consulted the list again. 'Rice Pudding Day?'

'Rice Pudding? Ugh!' Petronella shuddered. 'Well, in that case, I think the theme is clear. It's got to be animals.'

'In a zoo?' asked Sally.

'So, fauna is all right but not flora?' There was a resigned edge to Stuart's voice. 'Well, okay, how about an ark?'

Everyone looked at him suspiciously. If he meant an ark such as Noah had captained, then it was a good idea. However, there was a suspicion he might have meant the mathematical geometric type of arc. After all, he was the only one in the group who would think of the number 3.14 when anyone mentioned pies.

He assured them he meant Noah's Ark.

'It's perfect,' Sally said.

It was, indeed, perfect, and for the next hour, they discussed which animals to include. After all, if you mention Noah's Ark, most people picture popular animals, like giraffes and bears, not lizards and bats. But eventually, they decided they'd use all the animals in Sally's list of International and World Days, and add a few more different species if there was room.

'And, as a bonus,' said Levi with a laugh, 'if we knit some of the less appealing animals, at least the inhabitants of Creaping Bottom will stop asking which of our knitted figures represents them and stop pestering us.'

It turned out that Levi had been quite wrong

about being pestered. Not that people had asked which animal represented them because nothing at that point had been knitted. But towards the middle of July, everywhere Vera went, people enquired what the theme would be for the August topper. Vera told them and someone asked if it was a fundraising effort for endangered animals.

It hadn't been, but once the suggestion had been made, everyone considered it a superb idea.

'But how do we collect money for an endangered species charity?' Vera asked.

Stuart had taken over at that point. 'We can't put collection boxes around the post box because they'd soon disappear. But we could leave it up to each person to donate individually. We'll hang up QR codes which lead to several charities' websites.'

Beryl had a good idea. She'd been serving up the Cake of the Day – Cairns Coconut Crumbles and had suggested that as well as the QR codes, local businesses should be invited to bid to sponsor one of the knitted animals, like in an auction. The money raised could be sent to an animal charity. She'd asked if they could, please, include a koala.

'And whoever's bid is the highest for that particular animal can put a sign in their shop window to show they're supporting an animal charity. A win for everyone… Oh, and I'll put in a tenner more than anyone who bids higher than me for the koala,' Beryl said.

Things were getting rather complicated for Vera's liking, but luckily, Stuart volunteered to deal with the financial side. Thank goodness. *But wasn't that what a treasurer was for?*

Beryl's plan had been remarkably well-formed, Vera thought. It was actually rather exciting, and they would help endangered animals, too.

The August Noah's Ark post box Topper was extremely popular. However, as Vera knew, you couldn't please everyone, and various people were incensed by the omission of their favourite animal.

'What? No panda?'

'What? No tarantula?'

'No jellyfish?'

'No Amazonian green spotted tree frog?'

'Pterodactyl?'

Emails and letters had poured in, requesting – and even demanding their favourite animal be represented. Vera sifted through the emails, searching for A. Godbin's complaint. Would he demand a particular animal? Or would he simply insist she remove the entire topper? She couldn't wait to find out, but the days passed, and although Vera even searched her spam folder, nothing came from her nemesis.

She deleted the other emails, and after reading the letters, she screwed them up and threw them in the wastepaper basket.

Honestly, some people had nothing better to do with their lives. If they'd filled their Ark with as many species as had been requested, the post box would have subsided beneath such an immense weight of woollen creatures.

'Has anyone criticised us for not representing a Cocka-Loodle-Doo?' Levi asked and Sally guffawed louder than Vera thought necessary. On the other hand, it had been a jolly afternoon in Bonzer Buns, so much so, Vera's stomach muscles ached with all the laughter, as well as all the Cairns Coconut Crumbles she'd eaten.

But if there had been complaints, there'd also been thanks. Various animal charities had contacted them to express gratitude for their efforts. Apparently, people had been very generous in their donations. It was one of those days when Vera was grateful to be the chairperson of the group. The absence of communication from A. Godbin being the only minor irritation in what was otherwise a rather successful July.

At the *Tilly and Effie Private Investigation Bureau's* table, Tilly watched Beryl and the members of the Creaping Bottom Post Box Topper Society through narrowed eyes.

'Well, I like that! Beryl's congratulating herself for having the idea to make money for endangered species,' grumbled Tilly. 'But what about me? She won't pay me more. I asked for a rise, and she said no.'

'But you're not endangered, dear,' said Effie.

'My holiday is. I've got enough to get to Torremolinos, but not much to spend when I get there.'

Effie patted her hand absent-mindedly; her thoughts were elsewhere. 'Des said Alice still isn't back from holiday. He's wondering if she's done a moonlight flit. And if she has, then an unsuspecting neighbourhood in Southend-on-Sea may now be in danger.'

'Well, there's not a lot we can do about it,' said Tilly. 'Nan says it's peaceful now and she can sleep at night. It's a good thing Alice has gone.'

Tilly had an idea. She tapped her top lip thoughtfully. 'D'you suppose we should contact Tony Parstedd? He might pay us for the story, and we'd be doing the world a service by revealing the whereabouts of a serial killer.'

Effie shook her head. 'Tony Parstedd wouldn't pay up.'

'No, I suppose not.'

'And anyway,' Effie said, 'we don't have any proof… Although if we did…'

Effie and Tilly stared at each other.

'There's bound to be evidence in Alice's rooms,' Tilly said. 'And no one would think it strange if you got the key from the manager… Alice might have asked you to clean while she was away…'

'I might need a forged letter from Alice asking me,' Effie said.

'Would an email do?'

Effie nodded.

'Give me half an hour…'

Tilly and Effie arranged to meet at nine o'clock that evening outside Alice's flat. Tilly had visited her nan and left promptly a minute before nine. Effie had been to see Des and was a few minutes late because his budgie, Pegasus, had escaped again, and Effie had to coax him down from the curtain rail before Des would let her go. She took the key out of her pocket while Tilly, with head turning left and right, checked the corridor. The sound of blaring televisions blasted out of various rooms while Effie opened the door to Alice's apartment and let them both in.

Tilly and Effie sat in Bonzer Buns the next morning, staring at each other over their coffee cups.

'Well, the noises weren't blenders and choppers,' Tilly said.

Effie nodded. 'I know. There's hardly any equipment in her kitchen at all. And may I say, that Alice Gruber is a very messy woman. I didn't like the state of her kitchen. I can't imagine the germs she's growing in there.' Effie shuddered. 'But I checked the knives, and they were all blunt. Dirty, but blunt.'

'Blood-stained?'

Effie shook her head. 'Not as far as I could tell.'

'Obviously not murder weapons, then,' said Tilly disappointedly.

'No, but I was rather surprised at the workbench in the bedroom. It was very well-stocked, although there wasn't a chainsaw or anything obvious you could use as a weapon. A couple of drills, a few screwdrivers – nothing you wouldn't find in a tool shop. But the power tools could explain the night-time noises.'

'D'you think she was making murder weapons?' Tilly asked. 'There were lots of bits and pieces on the bench. It looked like she'd dismantled an electric fan.'

'I don't think you can fan someone to death…'

Tilly sighed. 'We're no better off. We've got no proof and I'm going to have to ask my mum for a loan for my holiday money.'

Effie choked on her oat milk latte with honey and two shots of caramel syrup. 'I just had a dreadful thought. There's CCTV in Hurrah House. Suppose someone checks it and sees us going into Alice's rooms?'

Tilly looked at her, aghast. 'Well, we didn't touch anything, so they'll have no reason to check the footage, and, with any luck, they'll record over it.'

'But what if they do look…'

'We'll just deny it. We'll say we've been framed. AI deep fake.'

'I don't know what that is, but if you're sure. In the meantime, we must keep quiet about what we found…'

'We didn't find anything. Except bits of electrical stuff.'

'That's true. Although, I was wondering…'

'Yes…?'

'That bit we thought was from an electric fan. It looked a lot like that UFO Ravi flew down the street. That groan.'

'Groan? Oh, you mean the drone?' Tilly slapped her hand over her mouth, eyeballs sliding from side to side over the top. Any talk of drones would undoubtedly attract the attention of those mad topper knitters. And that was the last thing they needed.

'Yes,' said Effie.

'Best we don't mention it,' whispered Tilly through the open fingers of the hand that was still over her mouth. Effie was right. It had looked like the rotor blade of a drone. Why hadn't she thought of it before? And why had Creaping Bottom suddenly become Drone City? 'People might start asking questions. And they might work out where we've been if we give away too much information. Best to keep quiet.'

This is a disaster, Tilly thought. Whatever Alice was making was bound to be lethal. Could she have been making drones? Drones with death rays? Drones with seek-and-destroy capabilities? It was all too awful to think about. Suppose Alice had her own CCTV camera installed in her flat? If she found out Tilly and Effie had broken in, she might send a killer drone to pick them off. Their bodies might be found, and no one would ever know who'd murdered them. Tilly bit her lower lip. No point mentioning that to Effie. She'd lose the plot. No, best just to keep quiet. In a few weeks, Tilly would be in Torremolinos. And perhaps she might not come home…

As Vera filled in her CBPBTS journal halfway through August, she had lots to report.

A superb topper and large amounts of money raised for endangered animals. Even the native animals of Creaping Bottom appreciated their friends on top of the post box. At the beginning of the month, during Vera's early morning walk to check the topper, she'd snapped a photo of a group of squirrels sitting at the base of the post box, looking up at the Ark. She'd sent it off to Tony Parstedd, who'd ignored it. However, it had come second in a local photographic competition and won her £50.

Still no word from A. Godbin, which was disappointing, but perhaps he was an animal lover and hadn't wanted to criticise their fundraising attempts. Well, she was sure they'd grab his attention with the September topper.

She listed the suggestions:

Something to do with Sudoku for International Sudoku Day. Stuart had proposed that. Well, at least he'd given up on the idea of flowers… Although Vera thought flowers might have been preferable to Sudoku.

Sally had suggested something for Teddy Bear Day. Perhaps a Teddy Bear's Picnic.

Petronella had wanted a celebration of Hobbit Day. Typical librarian's choice.

Levi's idea had been something to celebrate harvest with a special focus on crop circles.

But Vera was going to push for her favourite – Space Base Day.

Oh well, they'd meet later, and a decision would be made.

One thing was certain, Vera thought, *whatever they chose, it wouldn't be Sudoku.*

The Post Box Topper Space Base Theft

'I don't know what's the matter with Effie,' said Beryl. 'She's driving me barmy!'

The five Creaping Bottom Post Box Topper Society members followed her gaze towards the cleaner who was in the kitchen area of the café. Effie was filling in for Tilly, who was on holiday.

Beryl had forgotten – or perhaps hadn't bothered – to order a large enough Bonzer Buns shirt for her. Now, Effie's generous proportions were squeezed into a t-shirt, bearing the café's logo. She was wearing her own trousers and over that an apron that just managed to span her girth. The strings which went around Tilly twice, were just long enough to go around Effie once and to tie in a bow, although the tails were rather short.

The t-shirt, however, was another matter. The bun-eating kangaroo of the logo was so distended, it looked like a blue whale eating a boat, and it appeared as though the seams and fabric might not take much more. Each fibre was stretched to its maximum.

'She's gonna blow,' Levi muttered, unable to take his eyes off the cleaner who'd selected the long-handled brush from her Weapons of Mess Destruction golf caddy and was reaching up to scrub away at the corner of the café's ceiling.

Beryl rolled her eyes up until they almost

disappeared inside her head. 'She must've spotted another spider's web.' She sighed. 'I never thought I'd say this, but I can't wait for Tilly to come back. Fair dinkum. I know Effie is a beaut of a cleaner, but she's a useless barista. Yesterday, she whipped away a cup of coffee from Colonel Mustford's wife because it had a lipstick mark. A lipstick mark Mrs Mustford had just made on the cup after her first sip.'

Vera smiled sympathetically. 'She's definitely not herself. I've noticed she keeps dropping things. And tripping up.'

'It'd help if she'd look where she was going. I don't know if she's got a crook neck, but she's permanently looking upwards. She's so on edge. This morning, I asked her to take my electric fan upstairs and she nearly blew a gasket. She said she couldn't manage the stairs, which is strange because she'd only just been up and down – and up again – carrying the hoover.'

'Yes, I've noticed she's jittery,' said Vera. 'It looks as though she's frightened of her own shadow.'

Beryl nodded. 'Although only if her shadow was hovering above her on the ceiling. It's even worse when she goes outside. She puts her brolly up whatever the weather and drags that assorted long-handled tool caddy everywhere with her. It almost looks as though she's expecting an attack from above.'

'I blame her brother,' said Stuart. 'He's always

phoning her up asking her to come and rescue that damn parrot.'

'Budgie,' said Sally. 'It's a budgie not a parrot. Its name is Pegasus.'

'So pedantic,' muttered Stuart crossly.

'Well, Tilly will be back soon,' said Vera, who was keen to get on with the September topper planning meeting.

'I'm not so sure about that,' said Beryl. 'For some reason, Effie's convinced she's run away. Joined a flamenco troupe or something. What bunkum.'

'Well, my nephew, Lucifer, needs a job so if Tilly doesn't come back…' Stuart left the suggestion hanging in the air.

Vera looked at Beryl. Guessing she was thinking the same as her. Would the young Lucifer be a smaller version of his uncle? Or a worse version of his namesake.

'Well, let's wait and see if Tilly comes back from Torremolinos,' said Beryl.

Luckily – or possibly, unluckily – Stuart hadn't been able to press her about employing his nephew. A loud squeal from Effie and a clatter in the kitchen as she overbalanced and stumbled against the worktop knocking over a bottle of milk, called Beryl away.

Vera grimaced. That was going to take quite a bit of clearing up until it was done to Effie's satisfaction. Still, it could be worse, at least the milk hadn't gone over any of her society's members. Petronella still hadn't forgotten about the dry-cleaning bill for her coffee-stained skirt.

'Right,' Vera said brightly, rubbing her hands together. 'Let's get on with the September topper meeting.'

She read out the suggestions, deliberately finishing with Space Base Day. Thankfully, although everyone championed their day as she mentioned it, as soon as she said, 'Space Base', people's eyes lit up. Not surprising, given the television programme's universal popularity.

'What a super idea,' said Sally. 'And perhaps we could throw in a small teddy bear somewhere as a token to Teddy Bear Day?'

Feeling magnanimous since everyone had liked her suggestion, Vera agreed they could.

'And what about something for Hobbit Day?' asked Petronella.

Vera was sure they could sneak a Hobbit in there, too. After all, who, at first sight, would know it wasn't an alien?

'And perhaps the crew could make crop circles?' Levi asked.

'Don't be ridiculous,' said Stuart, and for once, Vera was glad he'd added his comment.

'Well, you did say harvest,' said Sally, 'which of course, is an excellent idea, so perhaps they could eat apples or sandwiches made from harvested wheat?'

'We'll see,' said Vera. Things weren't exactly moving in the direction she had planned, and she wanted to keep expectations in check.

'Sudoku?' Stuart asked.

'No!' everyone said in unison.

'I know,' said Levi, 'I've still got all the bits of that broken drone. Why don't we get Ravi to put them back together and then we could modify it to look like a space shuttle taking off and landing on top of the Space Base?'

Vera was about to put a stop to that line of thought when there was another loud scream from Effie. She'd fainted away. Later, no one could remember if she'd shouted, 'Groan,' or if she had, indeed, groaned. But luckily, she'd slithered down the wall and hadn't harmed herself. In the rush to help her, the idea of drones had been forgotten.

Once Effie had come around, Beryl tried to send her home, but she'd said she felt safer in the café.

There was definitely something not right with her, Vera thought. Still, back to the September topper meeting and the Space Base Day plans.

'Someone's going to have to be a bit more explicit,' said Stuart. 'I've never watched Space Base.'

Sally's brows shot up in surprise. 'You've never seen it? It's the most famous sci-fi show in the world.'

'Perhaps I use my time more productively.' Stuart tossed his head. 'Well, what's it about?'

'There are three crew members and a dog living on a distant planet in the Space Base and they visit other civilisations. They travel through space in special robotic craft that they wear.'

Stuart frowned. 'How can you wear a space craft?'

'That's the clever part. They each have a special "Shoot Chute" which they get into, and the robotic craft assembles around them. Then the Shoot Chute shoots them into space so they can visit aliens on other planets—'

'Sounds like nonsense to me,' Stuart said crossly. 'Haven't we had enough of aliens?'

Sally spluttered indignantly. 'But this is Space Base…'

"Bonzer idea,' said Beryl who'd arrived with a tray of sweet-smelling buns straight from the oven. 'I love Space Base. And, in honour of such a great show, I name these choux buns…' she hesitated for a second and then added proudly. 'Behold the Cake of the Day – "Shellharbour Shoot Chute Choux Buns". Henceforth to be known as "Shooties".'

Well, that had shut Stuart up, Vera thought, as she watched him reach for one of Beryl's buns.

'How about a topper featuring 'the Shoot Chutes?' asked Levi. 'We could have Perspex tubes and put knitted figures of the crew inside?

'Won't the wind blow them over?' Vera asked doubtfully. It was actually a good idea – if they could make it work.

'I could fashion something out of mesh that would present less wind resistance,' said Levi.

'It might be worth a go, it would look rather spectacular, just like the crew are being kitted up in their robotic space craft,' said Petronella.

'And I could put a sign in my window saying, Buy your "Space Base Shooties here!" Beauty!' said Beryl with a gleam in her eye.

Towards the end of August, Vera was getting nervous. Levi had still not produced what he considered were the perfect Shoot Chute tubes. They all appeared to be fine to Vera who'd long since lost interest in how aesthetically pleasing the tubes were and just wanted something that was transparent and would remain vertical in a slight breeze. She was prepared to do various spot repairs throughout September if it turned out to be a windy month.

The three crew members and dog had all been knitted in Space Base uniforms complete with miniature Space Base badges. Levi may not have yet produced tubes to his satisfaction, but to Vera, the knitted figures of the crew and dog were perfect.

The captain was holding the hand of a Hobbit and the mate was holding the paw of a teddy bear.

No apples, sandwiches, crop circles and definitely no Sudoku.

Stuart had, of course, felt the need to criticise. He'd suggested the captain, as the only female member of the party, ought to hold the teddy bear but had been verbally savaged by Sally and Petronella. He hadn't commented again.

If only Levi would hurry up with the Shoot Chute tubes. Vera began to wonder if perhaps Levi was somehow trying to incorporate crop circles in the tubes, but dismissed the thought as paranoia. Even Levi couldn't do that.

Could he?

Effie was finding it hard to breathe. Des had just phoned to say Pegasus was missing and could she come around to his flat and hunt for him. She'd explained she was covering for Tilly in Bonzer Buns and couldn't just leave when she pleased, but she'd be around later to help look. Panic was rising in her chest like steam bubbling through coffee. She hadn't imagined serving in a café could be so complicated and as soon as Tilly was back, she'd happily relinquish her apron. She couldn't wait.

Cleaning was her forte.

Coffees were not.

Although the cake samples were welcome. Beryl always needed a second opinion for her Cake of the Day batches. Effie had put on a few pounds since she'd been working in Bonzer Buns and that may also have contributed to her breathlessness. The t-shirt was too small, but Beryl had pointed out Tilly would be back shortly and then Effie wouldn't need to wear the t-shirt again. Effie could cut herself out of it and consign the remnants to the bin.

When Tilly came back… Effie was more inclined to think not *when,* but *if* Tilly came back. On the odd occasion she'd texted, she'd hinted she wanted to stay in Spain.

The person Effie definitely didn't want to come back was Alice. Des hadn't mentioned her having returned, so presumably, she was still enjoying the delights of Southend-on-Sea. Effie had scoured the Essex newspapers for murders but there hadn't been any for some time. Well, she supposed, even serial killers needed a holiday…

Effie hurried away from Bonzer Buns after her shift, with her umbrella in one hand and dragging her trusty cleaning tools in their golf caddy in the other. Thankfully, the sky was clear of death drones, although if she didn't watch out, she'd break her neck tripping up kerbs. By the time she arrived at Hurrah House, she was hot and breathless. Why couldn't her brother keep Pegasus in his cage?

Des opened the door to her with Pegasus sitting on his finger. 'Look!' he said happily, 'Pegasus came back to me.'

'Why didn't you phone and tell me?' Effie snapped.

'He's only just flown down from the chandelier,' Des said, his face falling. 'And don't shout or he'll fly off.'

Effie sighed. 'I'm sorry, dear. It's been one of those days.'

After tea, Effie felt a bit better and since Pegasus was safely back in his cage, Des was happy. After tidying up, Effie decided to go home.

Just as she was about to open the door, she thought it prudent to ask, 'So your noisy next-door neighbour is still away then?'

'Alice?'

'Yes,' Effie said nonchalantly.

'No, she came back last week.'

'Last week!' Effie squeaked.

'Yes.'

'But you didn't say. You haven't complained about noise!'

'There wasn't any. She's been very quiet since she got back from holiday. Anyway, why are you bothered? It's not like she's ever kept you up at night.'

She's kept me up every night since I broke into her flat, thought Effie but of course, she couldn't tell Des that.

'Shall I get Pegasus out of his cage to say goodbye?' Des asked as Effie picked up her umbrella to leave.

'No!' Effie said firmly, fearing another budgie escape and rescue mission. She wanted to go home – especially now she knew Alice was only a few yards away on the other side of the wall.

In fact, she needed to get out; suddenly the

Bonzer Buns t-shirt appeared to have shrunk, and was crushing Effie's chest. After checking Pegasus was safely confined, she hurried out into the corridor and closed Des's door quietly.

'Goodbye, dear!' Des shouted, too loudly for Effie's liking.

'Good evening.' The voice came from behind Effie, and she swung around.

There, poking her head out of Alice's room was the serial killer herself. Blood drained from Effie's face, and her knees sagged together. She gripped her Weapon of Mess Destruction caddy and her umbrella.

'Goo… good evening,' Effie said. For a serial killer, Alice appeared to be rather diffident. Was that her modus operandi? Lure unsuspecting victims into a false sense of security.

'I wonder if you could help me, please,' Alice said politely – almost apologetically.

This was very strange. Effie had never heard the woman do anything other than grunt or moan.

'Y… yes?' Effie wondered if her heart was going to thrust its way out of the front of her t-shirt. It might be messy but it would almost be a relief. The t-shirt fabric constricted her pounding heart like a steel band.

'I wondered if your delightful brother, Dave, mentioned that anyone had come to my room while I was away…'

Effie's knees sagged further. Did the woman

know about the night-time breaking and entering? Should Effie correct her and tell her Des was Des, and not Dave? Was it a test?

'T… to your room?' Effie whispered.

'Yes, has anyone knocked at the door?'

'Oh, no, no, no, no, absolutely no! No!' Effie said.

Alice appeared slightly abashed but relieved. 'Good,' she said slowly. 'So, just to be clear, nobody in…' She paused for a second, then continued, 'no one in authority came looking for me after I went on holiday?'

'No, no, no, no, no, no, no. Definitely not.' Effie was surprised to see what looked like relief flicker in Alice's eyes.

What did it mean? Was she really asking if people had been to her room to look for her? Or was it some weird way to let Effie know she knew Effie had been in her flat? *Don't let your guard down, Effie,* she told herself.

Alice continued, 'Sorry to be nosy, but I just wondered what happened after I left on my holiday. Shortly before, there was a bit of a… shall we say, fuss, in the village. A group of villagers running amok. I only heard about it, of course. Nothing to do with me… But I wondered if anything more had been said or if there'd been any follow up…'

Did she mean the drone chase?

'No, no, no, no, no. Nothing. No. Nothing at all,' Effie said.

'Good,' said Alice with what appeared to be a sigh of relief. 'Then in that case I won't detain you any longer.' After saying good night, she closed the door.

Effie leaned against the wall for some time, her heart thumping in her chest, complaining at the death-hug of the t-shirt. Or was she having a heart attack? She gathered up her things and on wobbly legs conveyed herself home, trying to scan the skies for death drones at the same time as peering over her shoulder for Alice creeping through the shadows in pursuit.

On safely arriving home, she celebrated still being alive with half a bottle of sherry, and fell into bed. But not before sending a text to Tilly.

I think we're safe.

A. Does not know about us.

Come home. Flamenco is not for you.

Effie.

Effie fell asleep, waiting for a response. For a girl whose fingertips were constantly in contact with her phone, Tilly was remarkably uncommunicative whenever Effie sent her a text. Why didn't she reply?

In the morning, she had received a reply from Tilly.

Wot?

What was the matter with a girl? Couldn't she spell? What did they teach them at school? Then, glancing up at the text she'd sent the previous night, she could see the reason.

I thik were safely.

A dousing know above us.
Come home. Flames not for you.
Efficient

Stupid auto-correct! Or perhaps it had been the sherry. With her tongue poking from the corner of her mouth, Effie's chubby fingers struggled to hit the right keys to convey the good news. And the plea to come home.

Vera called an emergency meeting at the end of the first week of September in Bonzer Buns. Luckily, there were few people in the café, although there was really no need for secrecy. Neither was there any need to give everyone the news. They'd all seen what had happened as soon as they'd passed the post box on their way into the café.

The topper had been relieved of its knitted figures.

The empty Shoot Chute tubes had been put back in position, but the knitted Space Base crew members that had been inside the tubes were missing.

What a disappointment after such a great start to the month. The topper had been an instant success. Space Base fans had descended on Creaping Bottom in droves. Unfortunately, some of them had ended up at Hurrah House, but after some confusion, they'd been redirected. Exactly how they'd known about the topper was a mystery, although Beryl had looked rather sheepish when Stuart had asked her if she'd had a hand in it. She'd vehemently denied it before rushing back into her kitchen.

'The thief must have been one of the Space Base fans,' said Vera.

The others looked at her glumly. Vera had been prepared for the tubes to blow over in the wind and to have to fix them, but she hadn't imagined anyone would steal the figures.

'We need to knit some more,' she said.

The others nodded wearily and got out their knitting needles and wool.

Several days later, Vera received an interesting email.

Not from A. Godbin. Vera had almost given up on him. No, this email was from someone who called himself 'Space Base Basil'. And attached was a photograph of three knitted Space Base crew members and dog at an airport. In the background could be seen the departures board. She forwarded it to everyone.

'Oh, how exciting,' said Sally. 'I wonder if we'll receive any more photos of them from other destinations around the world.'

The next day, Vera received a photo of the Space Base's crew and dog outside the White House in Washington DC. And so did Tony Parstedd.

He arrived at Bonzer Buns with a scowl, having been told by his editor to cover the story, 'whether he wanted to, or not.'

He obviously didn't want to, Vera assumed from his attitude. And guessed it was because he believed he'd been snubbed by not being included in the July topper.

'We've got to win him over,' said Sally while the reporter waited for Effie to serve him coffee, 'or he'll publish a really dreadful story about us.'

'Leave it to me,' said Stuart.

'Stuart!' said Beryl, leaping to her feet. 'You're just the man to help me carry the coffees and cakes to the table. Effie's in such a fluster today. And I wanted someone to try the Cake of the Day.'

Stuart, puffed with pride, followed Beryl into the kitchen.

Vera breathed a sigh of relief. 'Come on, Sally,' she whispered, 'can you do something quickly before Stuart comes back and manages to upset Tony?'

Sally brought a chair to their table for the scowling reporter. 'So, Mr Parstedd, how did you like the way we represented you on the July topper?'

Vera's mouth dropped open. She suspected he wouldn't like it much at all when he discovered he'd been the imaginary shark with the knitted fin in the knitted pond. What was Sally doing telling him?

Tony's frown slipped. 'I wasn't aware I was on the topper. Although I noted that most other people were.' His voice was frosty.

'Oh, yes,' said Sally. 'Guess which one you were.'

'Well, not the dogwalker because I haven't got a dog. One of the cyclists?'

Sally clapped her hands together in delight, as if he'd guessed correctly.

'Oh,' said Tony Parstedd. 'But I don't have a bicycle…'

At that point, Beryl and Stuart returned with their coffee and a plate piled high with Shellharbour Shoot Chute Choux Buns.

Clever girl, thought Vera, not certain if Sally had planned that or had been adlibbing. Well, thankfully, whatever the truth was, it had worked. Tony was now tucking into Beryl's 'Shooties'. And he was even smiling. A good sign? Well, they'd find out later when the Creaping Bottom News came out.

Overall, September had been a good month, Vera mused as she filled in her CBPBTS journal. The new knitted Space Base figures had remained in place in their Shoot Chute tubes on the topper. Space Base fans had poured into the village and the local shopkeepers had all done well, even Debonhair Styles Salon which had been recreating the distinctive hairstyle of one of the characters. And Ravi in Gadgets-A-Go-Go had sourced some remote-controlled dogs like the one in the show.

Emails arrived periodically with photos of the knitted figures of the Space Base crew in various parts of the United States with cheery messages. Vera couldn't wait to get to her email in the morning. She'd even forgotten A. Godbin hadn't complained about anything for some time. He hadn't been anywhere near as diverting. And Tony Parstedd, apparently a great Space Base fan, had written a rather good article about the wandering Topper figures.

And as for Bonzer Buns, Beryl had been baking Shooties non-stop all month. Sales had been so good, the Post Box Topper Society members had been allowed preferential mates' rates, which had brought the prices so low, everyone was beginning to put on weight. Next month, Vera would have to think of some way of getting the members fitter.

And, of course, they still had to decide on the theme for October's topper. But first, another cup of coffee and a few Shooties, Vera thought.

The Post Box Topper Celebration of Creaping Bottom

Life was looking up for Effie now she didn't have to look upwards all the time.

The air-to-ground drone attack she'd feared hadn't occurred and having lived under what she'd been treating as a state of siege for several weeks without being struck from above, Effie had grown fatigued. It appeared to be more dangerous to look up for a threat that never materialised than to keep an eye on where she was going. The bruises on her shins and knees proved that.

Another reason to be cheerful was that Tilly had returned. True, she was still as sullen and uncommunicative as she had been before her Spanish holiday. Indeed, Effie thought she was even more so since she'd returned – but at least now Effie didn't feel so alone in her knowledge about the serial killer who lived in the village in Hurrah House.

Thankfully, there had been no fresh murders either in Creaping Bottom or the Southend-on-Sea area. And, since Alice Gruber's return home, she'd been a reformed character. Effie's brother, Des, and Tilly's gran, Dora, hadn't reported any night-time noises. They hadn't reported any during the day either.

According to Des, Alice had even said good morning to him the other day. He'd added he'd never seen her smile before and had found it quite disturbing. But a 'Good morning, Dave,' was an improvement on the usual grunt. And he'd been too shocked to correct her.

The stay in Southend appeared to have mellowed Alice. Had it been something in the air? Perhaps she'd had a chance to unwind? Effie wondered if Alice had found religion. She'd suggested that to Tilly, who'd scoffed and said, 'If she's found religion, it's one of them cults what does human sacrifice.'

Spain hadn't improved Tilly's pessimistic outlook.

But as each day passed, Effie wanted to believe Alice had somehow been converted. Into what, she wasn't sure. But so long as Effie didn't have to remain on high alert, she was happy.

Another reason for Effie to celebrate was that Des hadn't called her to rescue his budgie recently. Pegasus hadn't tried to fly away for several weeks. Either he'd learnt there was no escape from Des's flat and that Effie would seek him down wherever he was hiding or he'd been too traumatised to try after her last rescue attempt with the long-handled feather duster. Perhaps he'd simply settled down and decided to enjoy life with his doting but absent-minded owner.

Effie's work had also picked up, and she'd now been engaged to clean many of the shops along the High Road, working early mornings and late nights. Her wages had almost doubled.

But if Effie was happy with her lot, many of the

shop owners she worked for were decidedly gloomy. And they were becoming increasingly fussy and demanding. Of course, she expected each proprietor to be particular about the appearance of his or her shop, but in her opinion, they were being rather extreme.

This wasn't Bond Street in London, it was Creaping Bottom. The slightest smear on the shop window or a minor irregularity in the symmetry of their display was often the reason for a childish tantrum.

Take that morning for example, Beryl had been very precious about the café's letterbox being scratched. Well, that was the postman's fault, not Effie's. She'd given it an extra buff, but there was nothing she could do about scratches. And really, what did it matter? It was hardly a health and safety issue. Beryl provided food and drink to people inside the café, not via the letterbox.

And Tilly wasn't sympathetic, selfishly only thinking of her holiday and the young Spaniard she'd met. She wasn't taking any interest in Effie's complaints about the various shopkeepers in Creaping Bottom.

What's more, every minute or so, Tilly's phone pinged as the young Spanish gentleman sent her a text. Then she'd have to translate his message into English and convert her reply into Spanish. She wasn't listening to Effie.

In fact, Effie began to wonder if perhaps she'd been over-optimistic, and life wasn't looking up at all. Everyone was moaning, and if they weren't actually accusing her of neglecting her duties, they were certainly becoming more challenging.

Beryl rushed into the café from the kitchen. 'Effie, there's a weed growing outside the café.' Her voice was accusatory.

Effie blinked and stared at her. 'I'm not a gardener, Beryl. I'm a cleaner.'

'Well then, I suggest you go and clean the weed away.'

Beryl's tone was so sharp, even Tilly's eyes opened wide in surprise.

Beryl rushed back into the kitchen and Effie followed her. This really was not acceptable. She wasn't responsible for what grew outside the café.

What sort of weed would prompt Beryl to such a temper? Out of curiosity, Effie thought she'd take a look. Stepping out of the back door, Beryl screamed at her. 'Where are you going?'

'To look at your weed.' Effie's ham-sized fists were now on her ample hips. Her dander was up. She would not be spoken to in this manner.

Beryl, however, hadn't noticed. 'It's not in the back. No one can see weeds in the backyard. It's at the front of the café in the High Road.'

Effie stared at her for several seconds. 'How do you know there's a weed at the front? You've been in the kitchen all morning. Did you only just remember?'

'No,' said Beryl, pointing at her laptop. 'Check out that email.'

Effie pushed her glasses firmly up her nose and read.

> *The appearance of your establishment, Bonzer Buns, is a disgrace. As I pointed out the other day, your letterbox is scratched, and now I notice weeds are sprouting up outside. I have no doubt that if this lack of attention is representative of your coffee and cakes, then you do not deserve to remain in business.*
>
> *Yours A. Godbin.*

Somewhere at the back of Effie's mind, the name *A. Godbin*, chimed various bells.

A. Godbin.

Effie nibbled her lower lip. No, she definitely didn't know anyone of that name. Deep in thought, she wandered out of the café into the High Street. There, in a yellow blaze of glory, was a cheeky dandelion that had pushed its way up between the café and the pavement. She glared at it. She did not intend to bend over and pull it up. Not even for Beryl. And her long-handled tools would only allow her to clean, polish, sweep or dust it. But not remove it.

She stamped on it. The root would still be there, and it'd grow again in a few days, so she hadn't solved the problem. But the next time she came, she'd bring some of Des's carrot wine and pour it on top. The weed would probably spontaneously combust, and that would be the end of that.

She went back into the café to finish her – now cold – oat milk latte with honey and two shots of caramel syrup and asked Tilly if she knew who A. Godbin was.

Tilly shrugged, her eyes on her phone. 'Nah.'

Like an electric shock had gone through her, Tilly sat upright. 'No, wait! Yes, I have heard of him…' She stared up at the ceiling for inspiration. 'It was that crazy, knitting woman who kept going on about him.'

'And? Who is he?'

'Dunno. She didn't say. Is he an old king? Or a singer? He's not a famous celeb, or I'd know him.'

Vera and the other members of the Post Box Topper Society arrived at the café for the October topper planning meeting.

Petronella had large pieces of paper and a thick felt tip pen. Sally had a list of special days for October on her mobile phone and, once they'd placed their order, they sat at their usual table. Vera called the brainstorming meeting to order.

'Do any of the special days leap out at you?' Vera asked Sally.

Sally scrolled through. 'Well, there's Halloween I suppose.'

Vera gritted her teeth. She loathed Halloween. All that blood and guts. Ghosts and ghoulies. Not wholesome in her opinion.

'Halloween's too predictable,' said Stuart.

'There's Harry Potter Book Day,' Sally said.

'Too boring,' said Stuart.

'National Handbag Day.'

'No,' said Stuart.

Vera's shoulders sagged. This was going to be a long and tedious session unless she stepped in. 'Any thoughts, Levi?' Vera looked at her ideas man and turned her back towards Stuart.

Levi was also checking the list on his phone and read out several possibilities. 'International Hair Day? Sheila Gote would appreciate that. International Coffee Day? Beryl'd like that.' He scrolled further. 'There are a lot of international days for really ordinary things.'

'Well, what's interesting about that?' asked Stuart.

'Many of those ordinary items are on sale along the High Road…'

'Oh yes. I see what you mean, Levi.' Sally ignored Stuart. 'World Egg Day, World Porridge Day, National Apple Day. They're all sold in shops along the High Road.' Her eyes opened wide, and she gasped. 'And look, There's National *Boyfriend* Day.'

Vera sighed. Trust Sally to find that. Luckily, Levi hadn't appeared to notice.

'Perhaps we could incorporate all the shopkeepers in our theme,' Levi said. 'It might give the High Road a bit of a lift. Everyone is so fed up at the moment. All I hear when I go shopping is people moaning about a customer making complaints.'

'But we'd have to make sure we don't leave anyone out,' said Petronella. 'You know the problems we had with the July topper when people thought they hadn't been featured? We don't need anyone complaining about us.'

Sally frowned. 'But will people want to be represented by an egg or a pile of oats?'

'You've got a point.' Levi tapped his chin. 'I know. Let's go rogue.'

Vera's heart sank. 'Rogue?' she whispered with dread.

'Yes, I mean why don't we celebrate International Creaping Bottom Day?'

'Because there's no such thing?' asked Stuart.

'Then let's make it so,' said Levi.

'I think that's a marvellous idea.' Sally beamed at him.

'So do I,' said Petronella. 'That way, we don't have to represent each person, just the village as a whole. I think that sounds like fun.'

Vera nodded. It did, indeed, appear to be an excellent solution, and far better than the ghosts and zombies she'd suspected they'd end up making for Halloween. And knitting with blood-red wool was so hard on the eyes.

'Excuse me,' said Effie, who'd sidled up to their

table. 'I'm sorry. I couldn't help but overhear. I believe you said something about complaints?'

Vera glared at Effie. 'Do you wish to make a complaint?'

'Oh no. It's just that I've also heard a lot of people mention they've received complaints.'

'And?' Vera asked. They didn't have time to waste on people's grievances. They had a topper to design.

'Well, I was just wondering if you'd heard of A. Godbin…'

After a sharp collective intake of breath, all eyes snapped to Effie.

'Only as I've been working along the High Road, that name has come up over and over with complaints about displays and…' Effie scowled. 'And cleanliness. As the Creaping Bottom cleaner, I feel I'm being unfairly maligned. Do you know who this person is?'

'No,' said Vera. 'But pull up a chair and tell us what you know.'

'Go to the Parish Council meeting?' Levi asked, aghast.

'That's the only way we'll be able to speak to everyone at once,' said Vera. 'I'm going. I'm happy to give up an evening, even for a dreaded Parish Council meeting with Prenderghastly.'

The corners of Levi's mouth drooped.

'I'm going,' said Stuart.

'And I suppose I'm going, too.' Petronella frowned.

Sally looked imploringly at Levi.

'Okay. Count me in,' said Levi.

'Me too.' Sally beamed at him.

The Creaping Bottom Village Hall was full on the night of the Parish Council meeting. There was such a throng that Reverend Prendergast's spectacles kept steaming up.

Villagers fidgeted and checked mobiles until Prenderghastly asked, 'Is there any other business?'

So many people shot to their feet, the vicar dropped his glass of water in surprise. He held up his dripping hands for silence and pointed at Sheila Gote in the front row, who was waving her arms. 'What is the meaning of this, Miss Gote?'

'A Godbin.' She tossed her head, crossed her arms and sat down. All those who were standing nodded and followed suit. Vera expected the vicar to ask for an explanation, but was surprised when he simply said, 'Ah, so you've all heard from that scoundrel, too?'

Vera narrowed her eyes and scowled at Prenderghastly. So, he'd also received complaining emails from A. Godbin? And it appeared all the shopkeepers in the High Road had as well.

Vera felt a sense of betrayal. She'd thought she and A. Godbin were exclusive combatants. However, that didn't appear to be the case.

How dare he? Waves of resentment like hot magma rose in her chest, threatening to bubble over.

'Excellent,' Petronella, who was sitting next to her, whispered.

Vera stared at her, detecting no sign of sarcasm. How could she possibly believe this was excellent?

Petronella whispered in her ear, 'With so many people looking out for our friend A. Godbin, it won't be long before we discover his or her identity. He or she couldn't give such detailed complaints without regularly visiting the shops. If everyone pools their knowledge, we can find A. Godbin and put a stop to this nonsense.'

Practical Petronella. As usual, she'd seen a sensible solution.

The HQ for 'Operation Find A. Godbin' was set up in Gadgets-A-Go-Go, where Ravi had offered to coordinate the CCTV footage. He intended to look for the common person in each piece of film.

Petronella had noted the dates and times of all the complaints received and had compiled a list of places where A. Godbin must have been shortly before.

And finally, by cross-referencing, Ravi spotted one person who was common in all the snippets of footage. Finally, he had an image of A. Godbin, Arch-Complainer.

Vera congratulated herself. A. Godbin was male, as she'd guessed. He was wearing a hat in most of the frames, so his face was partially concealed. No one recognised him. An outsider? It was hard to tell.

He was just a grey man who merged into the background. Nothing to distinguish him. Nothing that would make it easy to pick him out in the future.

He was even wearing a different hat in three of the glimpses of him in various shops.

However, they were closing in. It was just a matter of time, and then Mr A. Godbin's identity would be revealed.

Meanwhile, Vera and the society members were busy preparing the October topper. They'd decided October 15 would be International Creaping Bottom Day. It was a date halfway through the month and Levi had also discovered it was Stuart's birthday.

The date had been a wise decision because it ensured Stuart was completely engaged with the idea. He was basking in the reflected glory of such an illustrious day.

Petronella had been set the task of researching the village crest. There had once been a sign at the entrance to the village, but it had fallen into disrepair and faded. However, Petronella found several ancient documents showing the Creaping Bottom crest.

She held up a photocopy of the enlarged emblem. 'The sun, a heart and beneath them both, a bar with two semi-circles dangling beneath.'

But what was the bottom symbol?

Petronella laid it on the table, and they all peered at it.

'Handcuffs?' suggested Sally doubtfully.

Stuart screwed up his eyes. 'I think those two round, dangling things look like a lady's br—'

'Don't you dare!' said Vera. Trust Stuart to lower the tone.

'What? I was only going to say it looked like a lady's bra.'

'Well, it's not,' snapped Vera. 'There were no such underwear items in the day this was designed.'

'All right. Well then, it looks like a letter B that has fallen forward,' said Stuart, still squinting.

Actually, Stuart had a point. It did look like the letter B on its front with the spine horizontal and the curved parts hanging beneath.

'It looks rather like a bottom – male or female,' said Levi with a grin. 'Perhaps it's a B for bottom?'

What was the matter with everyone? Vera wondered. Why the obsession with body parts? She yearned to go home and take two paracetamol tablets. Then, she'd lie down in a darkened room…

'B for Bottom? Yes, that makes sense,' said Petronella. 'Sir Oswald Bottom. The "Bottom" of Creaping Bottom.'

Vera sat up. Perhaps it wasn't such a silly idea after all.

'Sir Oswald Bottom was the Lord of the Manor during the Middle Ages. He fought in the Crusades and is famed for bringing back a lion from the Holy Land,' said Petronella. 'Apparently, he called the lion, Hugo and it became quite famous.'

'Did it do tricks?' Sally asked.

Petronella checked her notes. 'Not as far as I know. Hugo is famed for eating Sir Oswald.'

'I bet it bit him on the bottom.' Stuart sniggered.

Despite the rather unpromising beginning to the meeting, it had ended rather well, thought Vera.

To celebrate International Creaping Bottom Day, they'd decided to re-create the elements of the village crest and incorporate some scenes from Sir Oswald Bottom's life. Not the part where he was eaten by Hugo, of course. That was too gory for Vera's tastes, even though it was Halloween later in the month. But some other scenes from his rather colourful life, according to Petronella's research.

While Sir Oswald had been away crusading or travelling the world, his wife Lady Bertha had languished at home in the castle. She'd fallen in love with Robert Grimbold, one of her servants. When her husband had returned, he'd banished Robert and forbidden his wife to leave the castle. Robert's brother, Peter – another servant – had formed a plan for Lady Bertha's escape.

Peter had suggested he fire her from the cannon on the castle ramparts. His plan had been to aim her at Robert, who'd be waiting on the other side of the valley. Unfortunately, although Peter was an excellent shot, he had no idea about range. Lady Bertha had hurtled out of the cannon but fallen short into the lake. And that had been the end of her.

Sally sighed. 'Oh, she drowned. How tragic.'

Petronella looked back at her notes. 'No, she didn't drown. Apparently, she was eaten by the crocodile Sir Oswald had brought back from his travels in Africa.'

There was silence for a few moments while the members of the society visualised the story.

'Right,' said Vera briskly. There was no point in dwelling on past tragedies. 'I think we have plenty of material to proceed.'

The October topper far exceeded Vera's hopes. Everyone in the village joined in with the inaugural celebration of International Creaping Bottom Day. Bunting and flags flapped and fluttered the length of the High Road in a riot of colour and motion.

Tourists came from far and wide. There was hardly room to drive a car along the road for all the people, strolling back and forth, buying souvenirs from the shops and, of course, admiring the October post box topper.

Tony Parstedd's report on the day had been front page news and for once, he'd given the society and its topper fair coverage. His report had been positive and peppered with cheery quotes from ecstatic shopkeepers. Although, Vera thought, his headline accompanying the sun, heart and drunken letter B of the topper was rather tasteless. *The Sun Shines Out of Creaping Bottom.* Typical Tony Parstedd.

The only disadvantage to having so many people descending on Creaping Bottom was that A. Godbin increased his output of complaining emails. Indeed, Vera received three during October, haranguing her for bringing so many strangers into the village.

Ravi was too busy to check CCTV footage for A. Godbin. He was making a fortune selling Creaping Bottom souvenirs. Unfortunately, one of his most popular lines was the Creaping Bottom Trilby, with the village crest on the front. All the shopkeepers agreed they'd put up with complaining emails from their nemesis while they were making so much profit. A man wearing a hat amongst crowds of tourists also wearing assorted headgear, including Creaping Bottom trilbies, was unlikely to be identified easily.

There was almost a breakthrough when Sheila Gote thought she'd spotted A. Godbin, peering into her salon through the window. Unfortunately, by the time she'd run to the door, the man in the hat was moving swiftly away through the crowds along the High Road. Sheila gave chase. She thought she'd trapped him when he turned off towards Hurrah

House. However, he disappeared into the woods behind it, and Sheila lost him.

An extraordinary Parish Council meeting was held at the end of October, and everyone expressed their thanks to Vera and the Post Box Topper Society for the inception of International Creaping Bottom Day. The village's economy had received a significant and welcome boost.

Typically, Reverend Prendergast assumed responsibility for the idea and insisted that the following year, such an important event in the village's diary, should be run by the Parish Council.

We'll see about that, thought Vera. *But let's fight one battle at a time.*

Sheila reported her suspected sighting of A. Godbin, but since he'd disappeared into the thicket, most people considered he must be an outsider. Perhaps he had a car parked somewhere on the other side of the woods.

But that was something to be considered in November when the crowds in the High Road and Creaping Bottom had subsided.

November, thought Vera. *And what would they do for the month's topper? Bonfire Night? Good heavens, no!*

Vera would have to come up with something good to distract her members from that.

The Post Box Topper for Remembrance

When it became obvious Reverend Prendergast was desperate to take over the running of International Creaping Bottom Day, Vera willingly gave way.

At first, she'd resisted, but as October progressed, she'd changed her mind. The society may have been responsible for the inception of the celebration day, but since then, it had taken on a life of its own. And not a life for which Vera wanted to take responsibility.

The Creaping Bottom crest had been resurrected and images placed prominently around the village. That was a good thing and had provided much-needed work for the village sign-maker who'd reluctantly been about to close his business.

The microbrewery in Upper Chortle had spotted an opportunity and produced a new beer – *Creaping Bottom's Up*. The village bakery was now baking Creaping Buns.

The members of the local amateur dramatic society were rehearsing a new play based on the life of Sir Oswald Bottom and his unfortunate wife, Bertha. It was called *The Bottom of the Lake*, which Vera thought rather tasteless since the 'Bottom' of the title didn't just refer to the mud beneath the waters, but also to poor Lady Bertha, who'd met her demise in its murky waters. Although arguably, not much of Lady Bottom had made it to the bottom of the lake, having been gobbled up by a crocodile on the way down.

Vera suspected the play had something to do with Stuart, whose interest in amateur dramatics had suddenly re-surged. He'd auditioned for the part of Sir Oswald and had been most upset to have been cast as the brother of Lady Bertha's lover instead. He was the one who shot her out of the cannon into the lake, where she encountered the crocodile.

'If you don't like your part, I could ask the committee to reconsider,' Beryl said. She had the part of Lady Bertha. Stuart had brightened until she'd added, 'They haven't cast the crocodile yet.'

Stuart had been strangely quiet about the production after that.

Vera wasn't sure if the play was a good thing or not. Time would tell and so long as Stuart didn't neglect his knitting duties, she suspected it wouldn't make much difference to her.

The local history society had published a book and the folk club had written a song that was rapidly becoming the anthem for the village.

That was definitely not a good thing. Vera thought the music was atrocious. One of those ear-worm tunes everyone hummed, over and over and over. She even woke up during the night with the song playing in her head.

There had been many other items of merchandise in the orange and purple of the Creaping Bottom colours. Bobble hats, scarves, mittens. Aprons – some with catchy slogans and others with rather vulgar ones involving Sir Oswald's surname. There were lions and crocodiles with nodding heads for the dashboards of cars. The list was endless and becoming more bizarre by the day. And that was mainly the reason Vera felt it necessary to disassociate herself from the celebration day. If Prenderghastly wanted to seize the steering wheel of this out-of-control juggernaut, who was Vera to remain in the driving seat? She'd *creap her bottom* elsewhere, as one slogan on an orange and purple mug proclaimed.

It would be a relief if people thought Prenderghastly was the figurehead. Vera could move on to more important things, such as the November topper. She realised with surprise she'd almost completed a year as chairwoman of the topper society and next month's topper had to be the best of all. But she wouldn't think about December now. She must focus on the current month.

To Vera's surprise, no one suggested a Guy Fawkes' Night theme, with pyrotechnics being added to the topper. Good. That would have been out of the question. Vera had no intention of being remembered as the person in charge of the society that burned the village to the ground.

The only suggestion – and the one that had unanimous agreement – was for Remembrance Day.

Very fitting, thought Vera with a glow of pride at her society's choice.

So, the theme had been decided. Now to design the topper.

'Well, obviously, it'll have to include poppies,' said Stuart.

Yes, of course, they needed poppies, but after the clumsy, chunky roses Stuart had made for Valentine's Day, they'd steered him away from knitting flowers throughout the rest of the year. Now, their topper design must include poppies. And if Stuart had anything to do with them, they'd be clumsy, chunky poppies. Somewhat reminiscent of red dog bowls.

Vera glanced pleadingly at Levi. Could he come up with a plan?

'I know,' said Levi.

Vera held her breath.

'Why don't we make one huge poppy to go over the top of the post box?'

Vera slowly let out her breath. That was actually a good idea. An enormous poppy would need to be fairly solid to give it some substance. So Stuart's debatable flower-making skills would be put to good use. How appropriate for the November topper. However, one flower seemed slightly austere. Was that a good thing? Perhaps it was.

Obviously, the others were in tune with her because everyone appeared to be deep in thought.

Sally was the first to speak. 'How about Stuart

knits the important part – the large poppy, and the rest of us make some small ones to go on top?'

They all nodded, except Levi.

Please, thought Vera, *don't change your mind and suggest we knit fireworks – or heaven forbid – use real ones.*

'Well, it's a fitting tribute for Remembrance Day,' Levi said, 'But I wonder if we can go slightly further?'

Uh-oh, thought Vera. *A twenty-one-gun salute? Please no.* She winced as she waited for Levi to go on.

'How do you mean?' asked Petronella, whose brow was furrowed and was presumably as worried as Vera.

'Well, almost everyone in the village has been represented on our toppers in one way or another throughout the year, except us. How about we knit ourselves?

'I hardly think this is the time to be thinking about us.' Stuart peered at Levi in the aggravating way he had that prompted everyone in the group to grit their teeth and narrow their eyes.

Thankfully, Levi wasn't taking any notice. His mind was elsewhere. 'I just thought we could represent ourselves on top of the large poppy, knitting small poppies as a mark of our respect, and to show how we are remembering those who serve to defend our democratic freedoms and way of life.'

Even Stuart shut up at that and there was silence for a few moments. Levi's idea of knitting the society members in the act of knitting poppies to show their support for Remembrance Day was good.

'Any chance I could be in it with you serving up coffee?' asked Beryl. 'Goonengerry Gooseberry Gingerbread,' she said proudly, placing a plate of the Cake of the Day in front of them. 'I could be on your topper serving up Anzac biscuits.'

Vera tried not to sag. If they included Beryl, the other shop owners would be jealous, and that had caused problems before.

'So, what d'you say?' Beryl asked with that *don't you dare say no,* tone to her voice.

Everyone recognised the danger of the situation. It definitely wouldn't be a good idea to upset Beryl. On the other hand, if they did as she wanted, they'd be in trouble with everyone else.

'We'll make a note of it,' said Sally, briskly writing something in her notebook.

Well done, Sally. Vera was fairly certain whatever she was writing in her book, it wasn't Beryl's name.

'We're trying to keep this topper simple, to show our respect,' said Levi. 'Although we could knit a few spare poppies and put them around your menu in the window. You could feature Anzac biscuits even though it's not Anzac Day, but I'm sure people will get the point.'

Beryl's scowl eased slightly, but didn't disappear completely.

'Well, I'm sure as mates, we can come to some agreement. Because mates get mates' rates…'

'Perhaps I could knit you serving Anzac biscuits

and you could place the figure on your counter?' Stuart suggested.

Beryl's face lit up.

Well, thought Vera, *that's certainly a solution, but not one I'd have come up with. Still, let's deal with one problem at a time.*

First, Stuart's version of Beryl was unlikely to be very flattering, and she might not want to display it. However, if she used it, then it could easily be removed before too many people saw it. A knitted figure could be knocked on the floor and lost, dropped in a mug of coffee… The list of possible hazards was endless.

And if people saw Beryl's knitted figure, and wanted one of themselves, well, the society members would just have to knit them one by one and take their time. But meanwhile, their coffee and cake bill wouldn't quintuple.

Conversation at the *Tilly and Effie Private Investigation Bureau* table nearby stopped as they both eavesdropped on the topper society members.

A personalised knitted figure of me, Effie thought, how lovely that would be.

Perhaps she could persuade Vera to make one of her. She didn't own premises, but she was as much a businesswoman as Beryl. The knitted figure could be secured to her long-handled tool caddy, like a lucky mascot.

At the first opportunity, when she had Vera on her own, she'd ask. Well, if you didn't ask, you didn't get. And Effie was determined to get.

Opposite her, Tilly was watching Effie and guessed she was going to ask if one of those fruit loop knitting people would make a figure of her. Tilly couldn't help smirking. Who on earth would want a knitted figure of themself? She certainly didn't want to be represented by an ugly, dumpy woolly doll.

On the other hand, she wouldn't mind having a knitted figure of Miguel, the boy who'd broken her heart. He'd toyed with her in Torremolinos, and then complained because she couldn't speak Spanish. Honestly, who in their right mind spoke Spanish?

But if she had a little knitted figure of Miguel, she could stick pins in it. Yes, at the first opportunity, she would ask the whacko knitting woman.

'So, Tilly,' Effie said brightly, 'if you have nothing more to report about the serial killer, perhaps we should end the meeting.'

Tilly shrugged.

Effie ignored the fact that today her teenage partner hadn't actually reported anything. Since she'd come back from Torremolinos, she'd been more sullen than ever and definitely not interested in fighting crime. It looked as though Effie was on her own in keeping Creaping Bottom's residents safe from murder in their beds.

But first, she had to speak to Vera on her own and find out how she could get her name on Sally's list to have a figure knitted for her. What would it take? A day spent spring cleaning Vera's house might do it. It would be a day well spent, and after all, there was nothing Effie liked more than cleaning. So, win-win.

The November topper was a gigantic success with its huge poppy on the top, into which Levi had inserted wire to keep the petals rigid. In the middle were five figures, their backs to the centre of the flower, each one knitting tiny poppies. Scattered around them were life-size poppies that Stuart had not been allowed to make. Luckily, he'd been too busy on the large poppy to notice.

There had been compliments aplenty, although of course, an obligatory complaint from A. Godbin. He thought their appearance on the large poppy had been disrespectful. Not a view held by anyone else, thankfully.

That was eleven out of twelve months of the year that the society had pleased most people in the village.

Vera had already started worrying about the December topper. That simply must be spectacular.

Effie had offered Vera a complimentary house cleaning voucher, and Vera had snapped it up.

However, Effie'd had to wait for several weeks before she could find a date when she was free.

On the appointed day, she discovered Vera's house was almost spotless. That wasn't surprising, because its owner always gave the impression of cleanliness and neatness.

Not that it mattered. Effie didn't let apparent cleanliness get in her way. *Her* cleanliness trumped *apparent* cleanliness. She'd wipe, polish, scrub or spritz with floral air spray even if a surface was immaculate. However, although Effie had set aside the entire day for cleaning *Chez Twinge* – what a ridiculous name for a house – she'd finished by lunchtime.

She also had a vague promise that her name would be added to the list in Sally's notebook, and if extra knitted figures were to be made, she would be second in line behind Beryl. But only *if*, Vera had said.

Effie hadn't listened. She'd carried out her side of the bargain. Now Vera must honour hers. Not *if*, but *when*.

Now what? Effie looked down at her long-handled tool caddy and imagined the small, knitted figure of herself attached to it. She wondered if she'd be required to do a sitting for whoever knitted her, like when you had your portrait painted. She hoped so, although she wasn't sure how long she could sit still. The merest rumour of a spider's web in a corner would have her diving into her long-handled tool caddy for her Web Wiper.

But first things first. What should she do now she'd finished *Chez Twinge*? Perhaps she should call around at Hurrah House to see Des. He'd been strangely quiet of late, presumably because Pegasus hadn't escaped for a while. Yes, she'd do that.

Effie stepped into the entrance hall of Hurrah House, and the hairs on the back of her neck bristled as she caught sight of Alice Gruber slipping out of the back door.

There was something ferrety and furtive about the woman's movements. Effie was already out of breath after her walk from the High Road, but now a surge of adrenaline shot through her. It turbocharged her across the hall to watch Alice through the back door window.

The Gruber woman was obviously going to do some gardening because after a glance left and right – but luckily not over her shoulder towards Effie – she went into the shed in the corner of the communal garden.

Not very interesting, thought Effie, unless, of course, Alice had hidden dead bodies in there. It would be risky, because somebody kept the gardens tidy, and presumably stored their tools in the shed.

Effie would ask Des. He'd know who did the gardening. And if it was only Alice Gruber who attended the lawn and flowerbeds, and therefore the only person who used the shed, she may well have dead bodies stacked from floor to ceiling.

Effie rushed to the lift, pressed the button and when the doors slid open, she stepped inside. As soon as Des opened his front door, Effie rushed to the window overlooking the garden. It was empty except for two women sitting on the bench reading books. Neither of them was Alice.

'Tea?' Des asked which Effie knew meant, 'Please make me a cup of tea,' rather than 'Would you like one?'

He'd already asked her twice, but she didn't want to take her eyes off the garden until she spotted Alice. Perhaps she was potting up plants inside the shed. It was possible. Did people pot up plants in November? Effie didn't know.

But eventually, after Des had broken a mug – the result of him clinking them together to attract her attention, she gave up and made him tea. Alice was nowhere to be seen, and Effie was parched. Before she left, which would be as soon as she drunk her tea, she'd go for a stroll around the garden. She might even clean the shed windows. Yes, that was a good idea, and then it would make it easier for her to peer in.

Effie went into the garden. It was now empty, so she crept to the shed and, with relief, noticed the door wasn't padlocked. If anyone challenged her, she'd claim she intended to clean the inside of the windows. Stepping forward boldly, Effie opened the door. She tried to suck air into her chest, but either her lungs weren't working or there was no air in the shed. Had her heart stopped?

Years before, she'd experienced similar feelings when she'd experimented with a cocktail of toilet cleaning products. She'd tipped generous quantities into a toilet, resulting in a choking, eye-watering green cloud that had whooshed out of the bowl and bleached all colour from the wallpaper.

Now, looking into the shed, Effie had a similar experience, except it would have been a blessing if her eyes had filled with tears. At least she wouldn't be looking at a dead body in the corner of the shed. Since she had no breath to scream, she just stared at the… Well, it wasn't exactly a body. It was more what a dead body might look like once it had decomposed, leaving behind a pile of clothes with the hair on top.

Areas of Effie's mind, which had switched off at the dreadful sight, now clicked back on. Shouldn't there be a skeleton? What had happened to that? All that remained was a pile of clothes and the hair.

Hair? If the skin had decomposed, would the hair still be there?

Effie was tempted to use one of her tools to give it a prod. Perhaps it wasn't hair but an animal nesting on top of the clothes? But she couldn't bring herself to dirty any of her pristine tools.

Hanging on the shed wall, however, she spotted something she could use. She nervously stepped inside and with the extended hoe, she slipped the business end under the hair – or the animal – and flipped it over.

Not an animal or hair. It was actually a wig. That would explain why it hadn't decayed with the rest of the body.

But now she'd removed the wig, it was clear the clothes had all been folded. Effie let out a long sigh of relief. This wasn't a case of a dead body at all. Simply somebody who'd dumped their clothes and wig in the shed.

And who'd last been in the shed as far as Effie knew?

Alice Gruber. And that was indeed the brown skirt she'd been wearing.

So why would Alice leave her clothes in the shed? Perhaps she changed into overalls to do the gardening? Yes, that was possible, in which case she could be returning any moment and find her clothes disturbed with Effie holding the offending garden tool. With a deft flick of the wrist, Effie tossed the wig back onto the clothes and patted it down with the tip of the hoe.

Best to leave now.

Vera had decided to keep out of Effie's way while she cleaned, so she'd gone to Bonzer Buns. Beryl was keen to discuss what her knitted figure would wear, insisting it should show her Bonzer Buns t-shirt with bun-eating kangaroo logo. She plied Vera with pieces of Shark Bay Shortbread – all on the house – while she made her demands.

Free shortbread? Well, why not? Vera didn't intend to go home and risk interrupting her cleaner for the day. It was best not to get in Effie's way when she was in cleaning mode. She was a demon with those long-handled tools. If your feet were in the way, Effie swept over them. If she spotted an invisible cobweb high above, the handle of her Web Wiper might almost remove your nose as it whipped past.

No, it was best to keep clear, and when Vera returned, her house would be spotless and sparkling. Vera looked out of the window at the post box with its topper in place. And there in front of it, writing something in a small notebook, was a man wearing a Creaping Bottom bobble hat. The same man, Vera was sure, who'd been spotted on various clips of CCTV footage wearing a variety of different headgear.

A. Godbin. It must be him.

Vera shot to her feet, scattering her notes and drawings of knitted figures. The rapid movement must've caught A. Godbin's attention because he jumped and, thrusting his pen and notebook into a pocket inside his coat, he hurried away.

Vera gathered all her papers together, shoved them in her bag, and rushed for the door.

'Oi! I thought we were going to discuss my knitted figure's outfit,' shouted Beryl from behind her. 'And what about the Shark Bay Shortbread?'

But Vera didn't look back. It was the choice between complimentary cake or A. Godbin. And Vera knew which she wanted served on a plate.

She hurried into the street, eyes scanning the High Road for the dreadful man in the bobble hat.

However, there was no sign of him. He'd hidden somewhere. Well, if necessary, she'd go into every shop and seek him out. Vera dodged in and out of shoppers, finally catching sight of him hurrying past the last shop in the High Road and taking the next turning. She broke into a canter.

Ahead of her, A. Godbin was almost running towards Hurrah House. However, he didn't go into the building, as she'd expected. Instead, he disappeared down the alley at the side.

Rats! Vera had lost him. Once he went into the woods, she'd never find him.

Perhaps she could follow his tracks? She carried on, wishing she hadn't eaten so much cake during the past year. She'd put on weight and was now huffing and panting. But when she got to the footpath – thank goodness – fresh footprints almost leapt out of the soft mud, pointing the way.

Trying to keep her shoes out of the ooze, she kept

to the grass at the side of the path, taking care not to trip over roots.

Ahead, she caught sight of something rather strange. A. Godbin was climbing through the fence into the back of Hurrah House. If he thought he could hide from her in there, he had another think coming. Two could play at that game Vera thought. However, when she got to the opening, she wasn't so sure.

Yes, she would definitely have to cut back on the cake. She squeezed herself into the gap left by the three broken fence timbers which were attached at the top but not the bottom, then got jammed halfway in when one of them slipped back into place. If she'd let go of her bag, she might have been able to wriggle in, but there was no way she was going to do that. It contained her mobile phone, her credit cards and, most importantly, her knitting patterns. She clung to the bag handles.

Calm down, she told herself. *Stop panicking and relax. Then try to force yourself through.*

Or perhaps she could dislodge another plank and give herself more room? With superhuman effort, Vera breathed in and urged herself forward. She shot through like Lady Bertha, erupting from the cannon, landing on her side and rolling into the hydrangea bush.

By the time she'd got her breath back, she'd stopped seeing stars. Getting to her knees, she brushed herself down, and, most importantly, collected her bag, then peered around the hydrangea bush. Who, if anyone, was in the garden? After the noise she'd made, most likely not A. Godbin. He'd probably have escaped.

The garden was empty. Other than behind bushes or trees, there was nowhere to hide.

Except for the garden shed.

He must be in there. Vera crept forward, realising for the first time, she was actually trespassing. Well, there was nothing she could do about that, and if she uncovered A. Godbin, everyone would understand.

Luckily, the shed door wasn't padlocked. Vera opened it and looked inside. Tools, old pots, a rusty lawn mower and, in the corner, a pile of clothes, and a bobble hat. The same bobble hat and coat that A. Godbin had been wearing.

So, that was his plan. Change into a disguise in the shed and disappear back into the woods.

How had he got out of the garden? It couldn't have been through the gap in the fence because she'd been using that. So, possibly, it was the same way that Vera intended to leave because she definitely would not put her body through the contortions it had required to break in. She'd simply walk through Hurrah House as if she'd come in the entrance sometime earlier. Patting her hair back into place, she hurried towards the back door, praying it wouldn't be locked.

It wasn't. Vera let herself in, glanced about, finding the entrance hall empty and, with a sigh, walked through the front door out into the road. No sign of A. Godbin there either.

Effie or no Effie, she was going home for a stiff cup of tea. That was not an experience she ever wanted to repeat.

However, she now had plenty to reveal about A. Godbin to the others, even if she hadn't caught him. The trap was closing and perhaps Effie could persuade her brother, Des, to keep an eye on the shed and see who came back for those clothes.

Vera called a meeting of the topper society the following morning. She reported her findings on A. Godbin. The others sat in silence, lost in their own thoughts.

'So, his point of entry into the village is via the woods. Then he changes into a disguise in the Hurrah House shed, walks into the village, spies on everyone, takes notes about anything he wants to complain about, and does the return trip in reverse order,' Petronella summed up.

'Is there a pattern to his timing?' asked Levi.

'Sadly, no,' said Petronella, who'd studied all the details about his comings and goings on her spreadsheet. 'It appears to be totally random. Sometimes even at night.'

'If he walks across the woods when it's dark, he's

remarkably determined to come to Creaping Bottom to find things to complain about.' Levi frowned. 'This isn't making sense at all.'

'And what a cheek using Hurrah House's shed,' said Sally.

There was a crash from the nearby table. Everyone turned to see Effie staring at them with wild eyes. It was hard to know if she was disturbed by what Sally had said, or that she'd made a mess.

'Hold that thought,' Effie said as she hurried off to the kitchen to get her cleaning tools. When she'd cleared up, Effie joined Vera and her team. Tilly was staring at her phone, thumbs a blur, completely absorbed. Probably unaware she was alone at the table.

Effie pulled up a chair. 'Sorry to eavesdrop, but I understand you found a pile of clothes in the Hurrah House garden shed. Well, funnily enough, the other day, so did I.'

After that, there was much fanciful speculation. Was it possible Alice Gruber and A. Godbin were in collusion? But why? Since the removal of clothes was involved, it was suggested they were having an affair. That was Sally's idea, but that made no sense. Because they hadn't had their clothes off at the same time.

Levi suddenly froze. 'I think I might have it.' The others looked at him expectantly. 'Alice Gruber and A. Godbin have the same initials—'

‘So?’ said Stuart. ‘Lots of people have the same initials.’

‘Well, I wonder if they share more than initials. I wonder if they are the same person.’

Everyone fell silent. Eyes screwed up as each person raked over their memories of accounts leading up to that moment.

Was it possible? wondered Vera. A man in Hurrah House who was posing as a woman? It sounded too fanciful, and yet Levi’s explanation was the only one that made sense of this rather preposterous situation.

But one thing was certain, A. Godbin’s secret was about to be revealed.

The Post Box Topper Shock Revelation

Vera didn't know which way to turn. The society needed to design a topper that would be suitably extravagant for Christmas, as well as a fitting finale to an extremely successful year. Furthermore, the design had to be completed with great speed.

However, there was now the unwelcome problem of A. Godbin. Vera had taken his email insults personally, and the whole unsettling episode required a satisfactory conclusion.

Effie had been on the point of calling the police but had been persuaded to wait for further developments. After all, as she finally admitted, there was no evidence Alice Gruber was a mass murderer. In fact, so far, there was no evidence of a crime having been committed at all. Two sets of clothes had been found in a garden shed, but changing clothes wasn't exactly an offence. And there were lots of complaining emails. But again, being cantankerous wasn't against the law.

And who would they report to the police? Alice Gruber, A. Godbin or both? One person or two?

However, it appeared that fate was on their side because at the December topper meeting, Effie and Tilly joined them, although Tilly remained engrossed in her phone and didn't participate. Shortly after Vera had opened the meeting, Effie's phone rang.

Vera drew in a deep breath and ground her teeth

when Effie pointed at the screen and, in a stage whisper, said, 'So sorry, I've got to take it; it's Des.'

Vera drummed her fingers on the table while Effie turned away and took the call.

Good gracious, Vera thought, they were wasting precious time that should have been used to plan the December topper. And it wasn't as if Effie was a member of the society.

Drum, drum, drum.

There was too much at stake here for chit-chat.

But if Effie had noticed Vera's annoyance, it certainly hadn't speeded her up. She greeted her brother and then paused to listen for several seconds. Her face lit up.

'Yes!' she replied to Des excitedly. 'I'll be over immediately.'

'Has Pegasus escaped again?' asked Beryl. She was hovering nearby, ready to serve the Cake of the Day – Fremantle Fairy Cakes.

'Not as far as I know,' said Effie. 'However…' she placed both hands on the table and leaned forward, excitement lighting up her eyes. 'Des has just seen Alice Gruber sneak across the back garden to the shed.'

There was a collective intake of breath. Then, without further discussion, the topper society members stood and thrust arms into coats.

''Ere!' said Beryl, 'What about my Fairy Cakes?'

Effie rushed into the kitchen and returned with her coat and long-handled tool caddy.

Tilly looked up, confused by the commotion, glanced about blinking, then looked back at her phone.

'Tilly!' yelled Beryl, making the girl jump. 'You're in charge. I'll be back when I'm back. And don't scoff all the cakes.'

By the time Effie arrived, puffing and panting at Hurrah House, the others had already gathered in the entrance hall. Levi was keeping watch through the window of the back door. He reported there was no one in the garden. Not surprising because it had started drizzling as soon as they'd left Bonzer Buns, and everyone was damp. Who would want to stroll in the garden?

It was decided that Levi should creep out to see if anyone was in the shed, and if not, whether there was a pile of clothes.

Levi returned a minute later, dripping. The drizzle had turned into a downpour. There was no one in the shed, although there was a pile of lady's clothes with a wig on the top.

'Now what?' asked Petronella.

They all looked towards Effie who pressed the button to summon the lift.

'Tea in Des's? We can keep an eye on the garden and make a plan.'

The doors of the lift slid open.

'I can make believable owl noises,' said Stuart as the lift rose to Des's floor.

Everyone looked at him in confusion.

'In case of danger,' said Stuart. 'I can make an owl noise to signal something's wrong.' He demonstrated, filling the lift with owl hoots.

'Right,' said Vera slowly. 'I'm sure that will come in handy, Stuart. In case of danger, we'll be sure to call on your services.'

Really. Sometimes Stuart was remarkably obtuse. But at least in this instance, his heart was in the right place. Even if his brain wasn't.

Once in Des's flat, they took it in turns to keep guard at the window.

'Whoever it is, they'll have to return for Alice's clothes eventually, and then what do we do?' Petronella asked.

'Oh!' Sally wailed, her eyes wide and anxious.

What indeed, thought Vera. Since she'd been the recipient of A. Godbin's complaints regularly for the last year, this – whatever it was – felt personal. As soon as Alice Gruber came back, Vera would confront her… or him.

It was decided they'd keep Des's front door ajar, so that when Alice returned, Vera could intercept her.

It was the best plan they could come up with.

'And I'll hoot like an owl if there's any danger,' said Stuart.

'Excellent,' said Vera. 'It's most reassuring to know you have my back, Stuart.'

'Look!' yelped Sally, who was on watch. 'Someone's coming into the garden through that broken piece of fence.'

Everyone rushed to the window to see a man in a trilby slip into the shed. Several minutes later, Alice Gruber, dressed in a skirt and twinset, and carrying a bag, emerged and hurried up the path towards the back door of Hurrah House.

Everyone rushed to Des's front door, which was slightly open, ears straining.

'Is she coming?' whispered Stuart.

'Shhhhh!'

'I only asked because I need to be ready in case I need my owl hoot—'

'Shhhhh!'

The sound of footsteps along the carpeted corridor sent prickles up Vera's spine.

'If you need any help, just yell,' Sally whispered. 'Gosh, I hope she's not violent… or armed… or—'

'Thank you for your good wishes,' Vera said, not wanting to hear any more possible threats. She opened the door and stepped into the corridor.

'Excuse me, please,' she said loudly but politely.

Alice Gruber jumped as she inserted her key into the lock. She turned to look at Vera and then froze. 'Yes?' the sound was a deep croak, like a frog with a sore throat.

'If you don't mind, I'd like a word with you,' said Vera.

'I'm busy,' said Alice, the deep croak rising to a squeak.

'It won't take long,' said Vera, striding along the corridor, shoulders back and head held high.

She'd expected a bit more resistance and attitude, but she'd obviously taken Alice Gruber by surprise and had the advantage.

'I'd like to speak to you about A. Godbin,' Vera said. 'And I believe you are the person to ask.'

Alice stared at Vera, her mouth opening and closing. Then her shoulders slumped.

'You'd better come in,' she said, but the voice was no longer high pitched. It sounded more like a man's voice.

Vera hesitated. Effie thought this person – whatever he or she called him or herself – was a mass murderer, and although Vera doubted that was true, it might not be wise to go into the flat with an unknown man, woman… or person.

'I'm not explaining in public,' said Alice, still with a deep voice. 'So, either come in or go away.'

Put up or shut up, thought Vera. Well, she'd put up.

Vera stepped inside the flat, and as Alice shut the door, she heard a sound like a distant owl being strangled.

Alice indicated Vera should sit down, and she perched on the chair; straight-backed, with hands in her lap. It was unsettling being in this strange person's unkempt flat alone.

Alice sat in a chair opposite. 'So, you want to know about A. Godbin?'

Vera nodded. 'Is it you?'

Alice, in her baritone voice, replied, 'In a manner of speaking. But you might know me better as Arnold Grimshaw. Back in the day.'

Vera frowned. The name certainly rang a bell, although having taught hundreds of school children over the years, that wasn't surprising.

No, wait… 'Arnold Grimshaw, you say?' Alarm bells were now ringing in Vera's head.

Alice nodded.

Vera had known an Arnold Grimshaw at university. A strange-looking chap who'd spent an entire semester stalking her. Everywhere she'd looked, there had been Arnold. Surely this couldn't be the same person? Vera peered at Alice, but with the wig, and the distance of many years, it was hard to tell. 'And did you study bicycle design and fabrication by any chance?'

Alice nodded. 'That was me. I am, in fact, a man, but for reasons that don't concern you, I prefer to present myself to the world as a woman, Alice Gruber. However, I was Arnold Grimshaw when you met me, and you broke my heart.'

'I hardly think that was the case,' said Vera. 'You asked me out once and I said no. As I remember, it coincided with an important rehearsal for the Operatic Society. It was nothing personal.'

'But I adored you from afar and you ruthlessly spurned me.'

'Nonsense. I did nothing of the sort,' said Vera. 'I think you're exaggerating.' Well, that wasn't what Vera had expected to hear. Was it some kind of joke? But Alice's face had fallen, and it appeared she was telling the truth.

'I was so distraught,' Alice continued. 'I asked another woman out and she later became my wife.'

'Well, there you are, then. It all worked out for the best,' said Vera briskly.

'My wife, Mabel, had an affair with her boss and fleeced me for every penny I had, so I would strongly disagree.'

Vera sat in silence for a few moments. 'Are you seriously suggesting that because I turned down your invitation to go on a date, your failed marriage is my fault?'

'I am,' said Alice.

'That's preposterous nonsense. I had nothing to do with it. Everyone makes their own choices. It's not my fault you made the wrong one.'

Vera peered at Alice in alarm. 'What are you doing in Creaping Bottom? Are you still stalking me?'

'Certainly not. It was just chance. You ended up here. Why shouldn't I have done? But when I realised who you were, I couldn't resist getting in touch.'

'Normal people would simply walk up to

someone and start a conversation. Not send complaining emails…' said Vera.

'Complaining is my hobby, along with making drones. They're the only pleasures I have now I have no friends.'

'I'm not surprised you have no friends. What a very vindictive person you are.'

Vera's gaze alighted on a drone sitting on the sideboard.

'Wait,' said Vera. 'Was the drone that attacked my post box topper your creation?'

Alice smiled nastily. 'Yes. I thought I'd discovered the perfect way to carry out surveillance on the High Road without leaving home. If it hadn't been for that Australian woman and her cricket bat…'

'Hasn't it occurred to you to stop complaining and start being nice? You might make some friends,' suggested Vera, although once everyone knew Alice was A. Godbin, she doubted that.

Alice's face showed she didn't believe Vera either.

'So, what happens now?' Vera asked.

Alice sighed and looked up to the ceiling for inspiration. 'Now you know all my secrets, I'm probably going to have to kill you.'

Vera leapt to her feet, a squeak dying in her throat.

'Oh, sit down, Vera,' said Alice crossly. 'I was joking. I like to spy on people and then complain about them but it's ridiculous to think I'd murder anyone.'

Vera swallowed. She wasn't quite sure what to believe.

'But I suppose in answer to your question, Vera, I shall have to leave Creaping Bottom now you know my secret. You'll tell everyone and I'll have to give up my hobbies.'

Alice looked downcast, and Vera felt quite sad.

'I'm very sorry if I hurt your feelings, Alice… er… Arnold,' said Vera. 'I had no idea you felt like that about me back then. Perhaps I could have handled things a bit more tactfully.'

'Well,' said Alice. 'You had your own life. No need to worry about me suffering.' His voice was bitter, and Vera recognised it would be no help if she apologised again. Alice/Arnold was determined to bear a grudge and obviously needed to blame someone else for all her or his troubles.

As Vera walked back to Des's flat, she wondered what would happen next.

'He's at liberty to dress up and behave like a woman if he chooses,' said Sally once Vera had revealed everything to the others.

'And he has the right to complain about anything he likes,' said Petronella.

'And if he really isn't a mass murderer, I don't have a problem with him,' said Effie.

'So, how do we proceed?' Vera asked.

'March him straight down to the police station as an impostor,' said Stuart.

‘Oh, shut up,’ said Petronella. ‘How typical of you to be so intolerant.’

Stuart harrumphed.

‘Perhaps,’ said Sally, ‘we ought to leave him be. He sounds like a very sad man with a miserable, aimless life. And now he’s not going to be able to continue his hobby of complaining.’

‘Unless,’ said Levi, ‘we channel his hobby in a slightly different direction.’

‘Not murder,’ said Effie. ‘I don’t agree with it. And I don’t want to encourage others to murder either.’

Levi tapped his lower lip thoughtfully. ‘No, nothing so drastic. But perhaps if he teamed up with the Parish Council, he could be their eyes and ears for the improvement of Creaping Bottom. If it was his job to find all those details that other people miss, he could report them to the Reverend Prendergast and his team. Then they could do something about it – or not, as they chose.’

Vera gasped with delight. What a marvellous idea. Turn Alice’s complaints into something positive for Creaping Bottom. And even better, they’d pass the problem onto the Reverend Prendergast. It was a perfect solution.

Vera informed Prenderghastly of Levi’s idea the following day. The vicar had been delighted with the suggestion and had immediately arranged to visit

Alice to put the proposal to her. Alice had gratefully accepted. It was enough for Prenderghastly to know that Alice had used the pen name, A. Godbin, for her complaining emails. The fact that Alice was really a man hadn't come up during Vera's conversation with Prenderghastly. And really, it was none of the Reverend's business, thought Vera. Poor Alice needed some privacy.

And now the A. Godbin issue was sorted out, back to the all-important December topper…

Levi had submitted a remarkable plan. Vera couldn't wait to tell the others of his proposal at the next planning meeting. Yes, the December topper was going to be spectacular – a fitting finale to the year.

Vera couldn't wait.

The Post Box Topper Christmas Finale

Needless to say, Sally gushed with enthusiasm over Levi's Christmas post box topper suggestion.

Petronella was very complimentary.

Even Stuart thought Levi's plan was excellent.

And Vera? She was spellbound.

However, Effie wasn't so keen.

'Alice Gruber? Are you sure?' she'd asked when she learnt of the idea.

Effie hadn't been invited to the December topper planning meeting in Bonzer Buns, but she'd hovered near their table, sweeping up crumbs with her long-handled broom, and had overheard the discussion about Levi's proposal.

She still wasn't satisfied Alice Gruber didn't harbour murderous tendencies. Once again, Vera explained there had been no evidence, merely much feverish speculation on Effie's part, to suggest Alice Gruber had murdered anyone. Unfortunately, Vera's logic didn't wash with Effie.

'Why can't you do it without that woman's… er man's… er person's assistance?' Effie demanded.

'I'm afraid that's not possible,' Vera said. 'And anyway, this is a private meeting of the Post Box Topper Society. You shouldn't be eavesdropping.'

As regrettable as it was, Levi's idea needed Alice Gruber's participation. And, in fact, Vera realised it was a clever ploy. As the official Creaping Bottom spy whose job it was to make a note of anything displeasing in the village, Alice conducted her duties with great zeal. Not that the Reverend Prendergast took most of the points in her frequent reports seriously. After all, did many of the residents care that there had been five yellow cars parked in the parking bays along the High Road when Alice had done a survey? This was not a normal range of colours, Alice had remarked. Was it some sort of yellow car owners' convention? And if so, what did it mean?

Prenderghastly didn't care if it meant anything or not. Yellow cars and their owners were not on his radar.

On the other hand, he was interested in Alice's report about the squirrels. They were multiplying rapidly. And what's more, each morning, they emptied a rubbish bin and scattered the contents near the churchyard. Alice had predicted it wouldn't be long before the litter blew in or was even carried into the churchyard.

The rubbish bin had rapidly been moved further down the High Road away from All Saints'.

Nothing was too minor for Alice Gruber's attention, and she wasn't afraid to state her mind. If the society involved her in the topper's design, then it would be done to her satisfaction and there would be no complaint to Prenderghastly.

Perfect.

Nothing must risk spoiling the last topper of the year. Nor threaten Vera's re-election next year to the post of chairwoman of the topper society.

Either the crumbs on the floor were particularly sticky or Effie was determined to hear more. She was still standing within earshot, brushing vigorously. *Swish, swish,* went the broom while Effie inclined her body so far towards the society's table, she was in danger of keeling over.

Vera thought it best to include her in the rest of the planning. After all, Effie had overheard most of the conversation. It wouldn't do if she talked about it to others and spoilt the surprise. If she was involved, then she, too, might feel invested and would be supportive. However, Effie proved a remarkably hard woman to convince that Alice should be included. Once they'd explained the entire plan, she'd understood and had given in.

Effie had also been carried along by Beryl's enthusiasm. She was so excited by the prospect of December, that she'd planned a whole range of Advent Cakes of the Day sweeping Effie up in the festive euphoria – not to mention the promise of a sample of each Cake of the Day throughout December if she agreed to the proposed arrangements. The post box and therefore the Christmas post box topper would be outside Beryl's establishment, and it appeared she was going to make use of it for promoting Bonzer Buns in any way she could.

She asked the society members if they'd put in a good word to Alice for her. Beryl was considering asking Alice to make a Bonzer Buns tinsel-covered Christmas Drone and had only been dissuaded when Levi had pointed out that a small flying object in a confined space might, at best, knock over cups of coffee, and at worst, maim a customer. Beryl had reluctantly agreed, but she was still toying with the idea she might have her own custom drone outside.

'Doing what?' Vera asked warily.

'Going up and down,' said Beryl, 'that's what they do. Isn't it?'

'But for what purpose?' Vera asked. 'People might be put off entering because they'll assume the place is under attack or wonder if a hostile foreign nation is snooping.'

'Yes, perhaps it needs a rethink,' Beryl conceded.

Vera breathed a sigh of relief. She didn't need any Christmas competition in the razz-a-ma-tazz department. Nothing must outshine the topper.

Vera's only misgiving with Levi's proposed idea was that December was a busy month, and the topper – once it was in place – was going to take up a lot of time. However, Petronella had already drawn up a rota and everyone had committed to participating.

Alice, with her absence of friends, had plenty of free time and she'd already agreed to be on duty every day. And that was just as well, because she was going to be in control of the show.

Would they be able to keep it up? Vera had no idea, but judging by the enthusiasm of everyone in the group and a few who weren't members, she was beginning to believe that perhaps they could. And if, for some reason, the show didn't take place one evening, at least the Christmas topper would be in place for people to look at. Or it would be, once they'd started knitting.

Originally, when Vera had begun reading Levi's proposal, she'd been disappointed. Not that there was anything wrong with the traditional Nativity Scene. Of course, it was charming with its stable, animals, shepherds, angels, and of course, Mary, Joseph and the baby in the manger – but it was rather predictable.

However, once she'd read more of Levi's notes, she realised how their topper would differ from most other people's Nativity Scenes.

It would start each evening just before the bells at All Saints' had rung at seven o'clock. Alice would wait outside the church, connected on her mobile phone to the society member who was monitoring the post box. At exactly seven o'clock, Alice would use her remote control to send a drone up the High Road with the illuminated, knitted star dangling beneath. Once the star was hovering over the Nativity Scene, the society member would let Alice know. She'd flick a switch on her remote control, and a beam of light would shine down from the drone onto the stable as if the star was lighting it up.

The show would last several minutes and then the lights would go out, and the drone would carry the dark star back to Alice at the far end of the High Road.

Already word had got out that something spectacular was being planned at seven o'clock each evening and various shopkeepers wanted to know what would happen. However, Vera had insisted on complete secrecy.

'But what if after two weeks of the star lighting up, people get fed up?' Petronella had asked.

A good point. Of course, during the past year, many people had come from miles around to look at their toppers, so possibly it wouldn't matter. There would be different people there each night, but perhaps they ought to have something slightly different the closer they got to Christmas.

'How about starting on 21 December, one of the three Wise Men could arrive suspended beneath the drone with the star each evening?' Stuart suggested.

That was a good idea and would certainly ring the changes. They decided they'd incorporate that idea, although it meant that on those evenings, the society member at the post box would have to unhook the Wise Man when he arrived at the topper. Later, after the crowds had gone, he'd be sewn onto the cap in a space that would have been left for the visitors from the Far East.

That led up to Christmas Eve. How could they celebrate that?

Levi suggested that on Christmas Eve, an enormous balloon filled with sweets could be conveyed beneath the drone to hover over the topper. Using the technique Alice had tried once before with extending scissors from the bottom of the drone, they could reach downwards and burst the balloon, like a piñata, showering everyone with sweets.

'And if they hit someone in the eye?' asked Stuart. 'We might be accused of grievous bodily harm.'

'He has a point,' said Sally reluctantly.

'Well, instead of sweets, how about gold and silver confetti? That can't upset anyone,' Levi said.

'Except the postmistress,' said Vera, who'd had words with the formidable Miss Witter before regarding clutter around her post box.

'Well, we'll rush out and clear it up before she gets upset,' said Effie.

At last, Effie was completely on board with the plans.

So, it was settled.

Now all they had to do was knit the figures and crochet the cap.

And rely on a lot of luck.

As soon as each member had finished knitting a figure, it was taken to Vera's house, where they were lined up on her dining room table. It had taken longer than Vera had anticipated because Stuart, who'd been given the job of knitting the stable, had been very slow. But finally, he'd finished. It was so substantial that it could almost stand up on its own. And much larger than anyone had expected.

Vera had knitted a white cap for the post box to represent snow. She was certain it hadn't snowed in Bethlehem that night, but who was she to go against tradition? Once everything was ready, the society members gathered at *Chez Twinge* to agree on the layout. Vera had been reluctant to invite Alice Gruber to her house but needs must. They'd look foolish if on their opening night, the drone didn't work, or the star didn't light up. No, a rehearsal was crucial and that couldn't be done without Alice.

Once they'd all gathered, they started arranging the figures. The stable was placed in the middle with the figures inside; an angel stood to one side of it and two shepherds knelt at the front, each with a sheep under his arm. Spaces were left for the three Wise Men.

Vera looked with dismay at the other knitted figures that still lay on the table – a whole host of angels, more shepherds and various animals – donkeys, sheep and cows. There was no room for them. The topper was full. But perhaps that was a good omen. 'No room at the inn' had been the reason for the figures being in the stable in the first place.

The three Wise Men also lay on the table, but they

wouldn't take part until just before Christmas Eve, when the drone would convey them, one by one, down the High Road.

Next to them, looking like a distended bladder, was the balloon which Vera had painstakingly filled with confetti. With pride of place, the star was in the middle of the table. It had been knitted with tiny fairy lights woven into it, and while Alice attached it to her drone, the others sewed the figures in place on the cap. Once everything was done, they toasted the final piece with mugs of cocoa.

Now for the rehearsal in Vera's garden. There were two more days until the beginning of December. Everything must be perfect.

As they trooped into the garden, Vera wondered if perhaps they'd been a bit premature toasting the topper with cocoa. Maybe they should have waited until after the rehearsal. Oh well, if everything went well, they'd have more cocoa and Vera might even break out the sherry. And if it didn't go well, it was going to be a long night.

They carefully laid the topper on Vera's bird table at the far end of the garden, and Levi waited nearby, connected on his mobile phone to Alice.

'Go,' whispered Vera, and Alice switched the drone on.

Everyone held their breath as it began to whir, then judder upwards into the night air. It hovered, dipped alarmingly, rose again and righted itself. After turning three hundred and sixty degrees, the drone carrying the illuminated star travelled the length of the garden until it hovered over the table.

'Now!' Levi said into his phone and a second later, a beam of light shone down from the drone, lighting up the topper below.

There was stunned silence for a few moments. Then everyone began to cheer and applaud.

Alice insisted on trying it twice more, but each time it was perfect and eventually they went inside and over more cocoa laced with sherry, they congratulated themselves. They were ready for their first show.

Tony Parstedd had been invited to the first topper event on 1 December, and it was hoped he'd give them some good coverage. Vera still didn't trust him, but if he was on their side, and his report was good, then it would bring people to Creaping Bottom to see the Post Box Topper Christmas Show.

However, on the morning of the first show, the Creaping Bottom News carried a sensational story on the front page. Margaret Bludge, a resident of Creaping Bottom, had apparently spotted a UFO flying over her garden. It had whirred, and there had been flashing lights. Before the UFO disappeared completely, there had been eerie shouting, as if aliens had been calling from their spacecraft.

When Levi brought the newspaper into Bonzer Buns that morning, they all stared at it in dismay.

'That busybody, Margaret Bludge, is my next-door neighbour,' said Vera wearily. 'She'd obviously been spying on our rehearsal.'

'Well, there's nothing we can do about it,' said Levi. 'Let's hope people don't remember the last UFO experience and link it with a Voodoo Doll on the rampage.'

Vera groaned. This was supposed to be the society's finest hour. Oh well, there was nothing for it, they had to proceed. And if the Creaping Bottom News had only given them a few lines on page six that no one would notice, well, word of mouth appeared to have been working well.

That night, the High Road was packed. The story about the UFO sighting and news of the Post Box Topper Society's show had reached many ears. It appeared lots of people didn't actually know what they were there for, but they had the impression something spectacular was about to happen.

At seven o'clock, the bells at All Saints' chimed.

All the members of the society had volunteered for duty that night to see the arrival of the star. Or not.

As the last chime died away, Vera heard the distant whirr of a motor and the gasp of people at the far end of the High Road. So far, so good.

Vera held her breath as she saw it. The star lit up with its delicate fairy lights twinkling. At first, it drunkenly wove along the High Road and then, following a more regular orbit, advanced towards the post box. In the darkness, the drone was barely visible, and it really appeared that the star was moving on its own. Children pointed in wonder and parents oohed and ahhed.

'It's a miracle!' someone shouted.

Vera's skin rose in delicious goosebumps. It was going better than she could possibly have imagined. And that was, indeed, a miracle.

Each night after that, crowds gathered on the High Road. They watched in awe as the twinkling star glided over their heads until it reached the post box topper where the brilliant white beam shone down on the stable below. Vera was thrilled at the success so far. Only four more days to worry about with the Wise Men and balloon. After that, there would be no more shows. It would be Christmas.

On the night of 21 December, the first of the three Wise Men swung beneath the sparkling star as the drone rose into the air. Alice had got used to the trajectory of the drone when it merely carried the star, but the extra weight of the Wise Man tipped the balance slightly and she was finding it hard to direct the drone in a straight line. The Wise Man's journey along the Hight Road was rather meandering and bumpy.

Stuart was on mobile phone duty at the post box and his instructions weren't very clear, so the dizzy

Wise Man overshot the topper and then turned for a second approach.

'Up! Up!' barked Stuart. 'No, not up in the air! Back up the High Road!'

Vera sighed. There were going to be words between Alice and Stuart after the show was over. That was assuming the wobbly Wise Man ever made it down to Sally, who was waiting to unhook it and place it on the topper.

'He can't find anywhere to park his camel,' someone in the crowd shouted and thankfully, everyone laughed.

At the same time, Sally grabbed Stuart's mobile and guided the Wise Man down to her, where she unhooked it. The drone rose and, hovering over the topper, the beam of light shone down onto the stable.

Rapturous applause.

Vera allowed herself to breathe again. Well, hopefully, Wise Man number two's journey would be less fraught the next evening.

There was much hilarity on the village WhatsApp group regarding the journey of the first Wise Man. One wag joked he'd been rerouted due to traffic congestion and suggested the two other Wise Men might be redirected via the M25.

However, overnight, Alice had obviously practised, and on the next two days, to the delight of the crowd, both Wise Men made it directly to the post box topper without weaving a tortuous route along the High Road or overshooting.

Word had obviously got out that Christmas Eve was going to be a special show. This would be the *pièce de résistance.* Three drones would proceed up the High Road, one carrying the confetti-filled balloon, and the other two with angels dangling beneath, like a winged guard. Once the balloon was hovering above the topper, the beam of light would come on and the scissors would plunge downwards and shower the topper and bystanders with confetti.

Vera was worried. She wasn't sure why, except that Alice appeared to be extremely nervous and that was enough to bother Vera.

Why was Alice so anxious? Although perhaps 'distracted' was a better word. Maybe Vera had underestimated how tricky it would be to control three drones at once. Had the topper society overreached? Oh well, it was too late to do anything about it now.

But if it was so complicated or difficult, why had Alice suggested it? Perhaps it wasn't anything to do with the drones. During the last week, Vera had noticed Alice spending a lot of time in Bonzer Buns, deep in conversation with Beryl. As soon as they'd seen Vera, they'd stopped talking and changed the subject.

Surely Beryl wasn't still harbouring ideas of having a drone inside the café? That was just a disaster waiting to happen. Vera's stomach sank. Alice looked very serious. Perhaps she was threatening to make a complaint against Bonzer Buns. That might cause problems for the society who were now working in partnership with Alice. Would Beryl remove their mates' rates? Or worse – might she ban them from the café altogether?

Vera would worry about that after the Christmas Eve show. There was too much on her mind now. She checked her watch. It was almost time. Members of the society stood around the post box keeping people back so everyone would have a chance to see. They also had small pans and brushes, ready to clear up when the balloon discharged its cargo of confetti. Assuming the scissors lowered and pierced the rubber. Effie was there with her long-handled tool caddy, ready for every eventuality.

Vera nibbled her lower lip and checked her watch again. The bells in All Saints' had started pealing. Five seconds until Alice at the other end of the High Road released her drones.

The entire street was packed.

'Go!' whispered Levi into his mobile phone, and from the far end of the High Road, Vera heard the crowd inhale. As the drones drew nearer, a gasp, like a Mexican wave, rolled towards them.

Vera could see a spotlight from each drone beaming down onto their respective cargoes. Two angels and a large glittery balloon. There had been a momentary panic earlier that evening when Vera hadn't been able to find the angels, despite there having been too many knitted for the topper. Finally, Alice had found them. Just in time.

Thankfully, all was perfect so far. And then, something strange happened. Instead of proceeding towards the post box topper, the drones veered towards Bonzer Buns.

'What's happening?' gasped Vera, but there was nothing she could do – simply stand there and watch. The three drones rose and the two conveying the angels advanced towards the café. Vera flinched as bright lights lit up the front of Bonzer Buns and Vera could see all the angels she hadn't been able to find earlier suspended as if flying. Presumably, they were dangling on strings out of Beryl's windows. There were even three of Stuart's angels which Vera had rejected because they were so chunky they looked like anaemic beetles. What's more, there were the left-over shepherds, donkeys, sheep and cows as well as several stocky knitted creatures that Vera thought might be kangaroos. They were bobbing up and down as if hopping.

The crowd oohed and ahhed, and then fell silent, as from Bonzer Buns came the sound of a heavenly choir singing.

'Ahhhhh!' sang the angels, drowning out Vera's screech as she realised everything was sliding out of control.

The balloon had retreated from Bonzer Buns and was now hovering over the post box topper. Slowly, the scissors descended, piercing the balloon and showering everyone with gold and silver pieces while the crowd applauded wildly.

Effie rushed forward with her long-handled brush and pan and swept vigorously as the crowd continued to cheer. Vera looked up at Beryl's illuminated café, with its shepherds, angels, farm animals and mutant kangaroos, who appeared to be serenading them with heavenly sounds. She watched spellbound, unsure whether the topper had been outdone by Bonzer Buns or whether the angels, shepherds and kangaroos had added to the entire show.

Before she could make up her mind, abruptly the choir finished, and everything was plunged into darkness. Then, a blaze of light shone from inside Bonzer Buns, including the neon sign in the window proclaiming it was open. People charged into the café where Beryl and Tilly, wearing Santa Claus hats, were waiting to serve them.

'So, that's why Alice had spent so much time in Bonzer Buns on the run-up to Christmas Eve. We've been hijacked,' Vera gasped.

Sally turned to Stuart. 'You knitted those kangaroos, didn't you?'

Even in the darkness, Vera could tell Stuart was blushing.

'How did you know?' But before anyone could tell him, he added, 'Well anyway, you'll be pleased to know that for the rest of the year, we have treble mate's rates in Bonzer Buns thanks to my assistance.'

That was good news, but still, Vera's pride was dented. Right at the final moment, Beryl had stolen the show.

'Excuse me…' It was Tony Parstedd. 'Could you people please stand near your topper? I'd like to take a photo. This will be on the front page tomorrow.' He shepherded the members to the post box. 'Now, could one of you throw some of that confetti up in the air so it flutters down as I take the photos?'

'Oh, for goodness' sake,' said Effie, 'I just cleaned that all up.'

Tony Parstedd's photographs in the Creaping Bottom News were amazing. They showed a merry group of society members being showered with confetti and standing by their Christmas post box topper. His report was glowing and although Bonzer Buns was mentioned, it was portrayed as the backdrop to the topper.

Things couldn't have gone better, thought Vera, and she toasted the Christmas topper with a mug of cocoa and a splash of sherry.

Now to consider the January topper, although arguably, it might not be her responsibility to decide. At the next meeting, the members would vote in the new chair and Vera wasn't sure who might be voted in, but a warm glow inside suggested it might be her.

The Post Box Topper Society Chairperson

Vera had planned to hold the vote for the society's chairperson for 2024 at the beginning of the January topper planning meeting. Whoever was voted in – and Vera desperately hoped it would be her – would then be responsible for deciding on the January topper. However, December had been so hectic with the nightly shows, she hadn't been able to arrange a time when everyone could attend. They risked having nothing prepared for 1 January. And that was unthinkable.

Eventually, the decision about the topper had been made by email with Levi proposing a large, almost sculptural head of the Roman god, Janus. The two-faced god had given his name to January and Levi had suggested one face peer up the High Road towards All Saints' and the other face down the High Road towards the village green.

He'd volunteered to knit or crochet the head – whichever worked best – and suggested they surround the bust with January flowers, perhaps carnations and snowdrops. Stuart had been asked to knit garnets, January's gemstone. Vera had smiled when she'd read Levi's suggestion. His garnets might look like deflated balls but would surely be more realistic than his attempts at flowers.

The vote for the chairperson would have to wait

until they could all agree on a date to meet. Vera consoled herself with the thought she'd remain in position until that happened, although she wasn't sure how she was going to curb her nerves until then. Suppose someone else was voted in and she was discarded?

Common sense told her she'd still be part of the society, but her pride would take a severe denting. Being the chairperson gave Vera something to get up for in the morning. She *needed* her position.

And before she'd know if she'd retain it, she had to put up with her sister, Felicity, who was coming to stay over Christmas. Not only that, but Felicity would bring her snappy, yappy terrier, Toulouse-Lautrec.

The end of December loomed grey and miserable.

And while she fretted, all the other members of the society were preoccupied with their own lives. Petronella had heard she'd been promoted to head librarian and alternated between excitement and apprehension.

Levi's central heating had broken, and Sally had invited him to stay in her flat over Christmas. When Vera had heard this, she'd sighed and sent silent waves of commiseration to Sally, who would pin her hopes on finally winning Levi's heart. A doomed cause. And yet, despite Vera's misgivings and Levi's previous imperviousness to Sally's charms, they appeared to have achieved a new closeness. Could Levi have finally fallen for Sally? That would be a fairy tale ending to the year.

Insensitive Stuart would have been the last person Vera would have turned to for sympathy, but even he was preoccupied. Of all people, he was spending a lot of time with Alice. It appeared they were both interested in investing in cryptocurrency and were busy comparing research. Well, so long as Stuart didn't invest any of the society's funds in anything Vera couldn't see or touch, she wasn't worried.

Beryl was engrossed in new recipes for the coming year and Effie was giving Des's flat an early spring clean. No one was interested in Vera's worries.

At last. Vera hung the new calendar up and breathed a sigh of relief as she waved goodbye to Felicity and Toulouse-Lautrec. Christmas had been excruciating, but it was over, and the new year had begun.

January first.

What would it bring? Vera would find out shortly at the meeting in Bonzer Buns. They'd agreed to meet at the post box and install the January topper. It would be the first time Vera had seen Janus and she was eager to discover what Levi had created. She gathered up her knitted carnations and set off for the High Road.

Levi and Sally had arrived before Vera and placed the knitted Janus in position. He was a work of art, with a human-sized head and two different faces. Petronella rushed up, out of breath, having lost track of time and once the carnations and snowdrops had been attached, Stuart arrived with his knitted garnets.

Vera would have been hard-pressed to identify them if she hadn't known what they were. Beanbags came to mind.

'Oh, look,' a woman pushing a shopping trolley remarked to her friend as they walked past with necks craning. 'Those red things are haggis. It's the topper for January, you know,' she added knowledgeably.

'Who's the big head?' the other one asked.

'Must be Robbie Burns, I expect.'

'Why's he got two faces, then?'

By that time, the two women were out of earshot and Vera could hear no more. Oh well, she wasn't responsible for people's lack of general knowledge.

By that time, the garnets had been fixed to the topper and if nobody recognised them well, they were a welcome splash of red to the pinks and white of the flowers.

'Coffee?' asked Levi once they'd approved the arrangement of everything and taken photos.

All the members followed him into Bonzer Buns.

This is it, thought Vera. My life is about to be decided for me. If only everyone was taking it as seriously as her.

Once they'd been served with their selection of Beryl's coffees and her Cake of the Day – A Brownie Like Alice – Vera cleared her throat and nervously opened the meeting.

No one took any notice.

Sally and Levi were staring into each other's eyes, Petronella was peering at her mobile phone, Effie was attacking a spider web that had appeared overnight in the corner and Stuart waved to Alice who'd just entered the café.

'What can I get you, Alice?' Beryl asked.

Vera's jaw dropped. She'd lost everyone's respect. That could mean only one thing.

Alice ordered and everyone looked at Levi expectantly.

So, thought Vera. Levi has taken over. She sighed and hoped she could control her bottom lip, which had begun to quiver.

'Right,' said Levi. 'It looks like everyone is here, so I'll show you all the final part of the January topper.'

Vera looked outside at Janus peering up and down the High Road. She'd thought it was complete.

'Surprise!' said Sally as she and Levi took out several other knitted objects and laid them on the table. 'One for each of us. We're going to sew each one on the outside of the cap to dangle down.'

'This is for Alice,' Levi said, placing a silver knitted drone on the table. 'And this is for Petronella. Creaping Bottom's new head librarian.'

It was a knitted book. Petronella picked it up and admired it.

'This is for our treasurer, Stuart,' Levi said, placing a silver knitted coin next to the book.

'The cupcake is for Beryl, who keeps us fed. And the broom is, of course, for Effie, who keeps us clean,' Sally said with a laugh. 'And this is for Levi, the man with all the ideas.' She placed a knitted paintbrush next to the cake and beamed at him.

Smiling soppily at Sally, Levi said, 'This is for Sally who is always thinking of others.' He placed a red heart next to the paintbrush.

One for each of them. Vera paused. Nothing for her. Was this their way of telling her she was no longer needed? She started to rise. There was no point staying if she wasn't wanted and anyway, tears were close. She didn't want to show herself up.

'And this one is for Vera,' Sally said, her smile huge.

She held up a knitted, straight-backed chair. 'A chair for our chairperson.'

The breath caught in Vera's throat. 'Ch… chairperson?'

'Of course,' said Levi. 'Who else could run the society?'

'B… but don't we need to vote?' Vera asked.

Heads shook all around the table.

'A waste of time,' said Stuart with a shrug. 'There couldn't possibly be anyone else at the helm.'

'And just to celebrate,' said Beryl, revealing a pyramid of cakes on a tray, 'Twinge Treacle Tarts.'

'Another Cake of the Day?' Petronella asked.

'No,' said Beryl. 'These are Cake of the Year.'

About the Author

Dawn spent much of her childhood making up stories filled with romance, drama and excitement. She loved fairy tales, although if she cast herself as a character, she'd more likely have played the part of the Court Jester than the Princess. She didn't recognise it at the time, but she was searching for the emotional depth in the stories she read. It wasn't enough to be told the Prince loved the Princess, she wanted to know how he felt and to see him declare his love. She wanted to see the wedding. And so she'd furnish her stories with those details.

Nowadays, she hopes to write books that will engage readers' passions. From poignant stories set during the First World War, to the zany antics of the inhabitants of the fictitious town of Basilwade; and from historical romances to the fantasy adventures of a group of anthropomorphic animals led by a chicken with delusions of grandeur, she explores the richness and depth of human emotion.

A book by Dawn will offer laughter or tears – or anything in between, but if she touches your soul, she'll consider her job well done.

She has been a finalist in the Wishing Shelf Book Awards for 2017 and 2020, Readers' Favorite Book Awards 2018 and Independent Author Network Book of the Year Award 2018.

Dawn has also written two plays about the First

World War, which have been performed in England, Germany and France.

If you'd like to read an exclusive prequel and sequel to *The Post Box Topper Chronicles*, as well as free stories and added information about her books, please sign up to Dawn's email newsletter on her blog: https://dawnknox.com

The Basilwade Chronicles can be found here: https://mybook.to/TheBasilwadeChronicles

The Duchess of Sydney can be found here: https://mybook.to/TheDuchessOfSydney

A Cottage in Plotlands can be found here: https://mybook.to/ACottageInPlotlands

Like to Read More Work Like This?

Then sign up to our mailing list and download our free collection of short stories, *Magnetism*. Sign up now to receive this free e-book and also to find out about all of our new publications and offers.

Sign up here:
http://eepurl.com/gbpdVz

Please Leave a Review

Reviews are so important to writers. Please take the time to review this book. A couple of lines is fine.

Reviews help the book to become more visible to buyers. Retailers will promote books with multiple reviews.

This in turn helps us to sell more books... And then we can afford to publish more books like this one.

Leaving a review is very easy.

Go to https://amzn.to/3zQzdk9, scroll down the left-hand side of the Amazon page and click on the 'Write a customer review' button.

Other Writing by Dawn Knox

The Basilwade Chronicles

Published by Chapeltown

The Basilwade stories were originally published on the CaféLit website, where you can access short stories that go nicely with a cuppa. We even suggest a drink! Dawn Knox's stories contain characters and situations that may seem a little larger than life at first glance but we can soon see that everyone involved is very human. And don't we all recognise the quirkiness of village/small-town life?.

'It's been a long time since I spent so much of my time laughing while reading a book. Endlessly inventive, crackling jokes, no two characters alike. And every story ends, not with a cliffhanger or a hook into the next one, but the eager need to answer the question, "NOW WHAT HAPPENS?"

'If Basilwade doesn't actually exist somewhere, it thoroughly deserves to!' (*Amazon*)

Order from Amazon:

Paperback: ISBN 978-1-910542-49-1
eBook: ISBN 978-1-910542-47-7

Chapeltown Books

The Crispin Chronicles

Published by Chapeltown

Goings on in the Garden.

Join Crispin, the Marble Elf, in Her Ladyship's secret, fantastical Garden, where Gnomes, Cockney Leprechauns, Cherubs, Trolls and Pole-Dancing Fairies live, love and laugh. But watch out for the Shed of No Return – the clue is in the name. And keep upwind of the begonias where Gusty Bob, the flatulent Toad is usually found. Oh, and don't trip over the Wooden Robin; he's likely to stop at short notice to pull up his socks.

'This is a good read with plenty of entertaining characters and humorous incidents. I would definitely recommend this if you need cheering up.' (*Amazon*)

Order from Amazon:

Paperback: ISBN 978-1-910542-87-3
eBook: ISBN 978-1-910542-88-0

Chapeltown Books

Printed in Great Britain
by Amazon

45137301R00119